FIGHT FOR HOME

WAY HOME SERIES BOOK TWO

KIM MILLS

The Fight for Home
Copyright © 2018 Kim Mills
All Rights Reserved
The Fight for Home is a work of fiction. Names, characters, businesses, places, events and incidents are all the products of the author's imagination.
Except Canadian Infantry Officers. They exist, I swear.
Any resemblance to actual persons, living or dead, or actual events is purely coincidental.
Even if you think it's about you, it's not.

Front cover designed by **designrans**

Editing by Susan Soares: SJS Editorial Services

Illustrations by Dh
(There are still no illustrations)

This book is dedicated to the many, many military spouses who came before me, especially the ones who taught me what real strength looks like.
I only stand here today because you showed me how.

Love is when you have 100 reasons to leave someone, but you still look for one reason to fight for them.

~ Unknown

1

MARK

PRESENT

The hallway is sterile, the smell that strange combination of sweet and sickly, filthy and sanitized. There are no happy moments here. No one is smiling, or laughing, or even really speaking in any more than a hushed whisper. Instead, everyone who does look up as I walk by doesn't even change their expression. They assume there's nothing about me that's different from anyone else here. We're all walking these halls wishing we were anywhere else. No one meets my eye.

They're wrong, though, about one thing. It's true I'd rather not be here, but I am different from the rest. The rest of these visitors, they've been here from the beginning. I bet they rushed in, mere moments after their loved ones arrived. I bet they've been holding hands and hair, and comforting tears from that very first moment things went wrong. That's what you do, when someone you love is sick.

But that's not what I've done. This is my first walk down this hall. The first time I've found parking and pressed on a visitor sticker. My nose isn't accustomed to the smell in here, and my ears haven't yet blocked out the hum of the fluorescent lights. I wonder if some of these people even notice the one at the end of the hall flickers. I bet they've been here so often they've stopped seeing it.

I do, though.

I see it.

The nurse coming out of her room knows it, too. As I stand here, staring at the name written hastily on the whiteboard outside this door, she looks at me, long and hard. I have no excuse. I should have been here. I should have been here weeks ago. I shouldn't be reading a worn, smudged chart. I should know everything written here.

I should already be used to these lights and that smell.

The nurse's smile is forced as she sizes me up before looking me in the eyes. These halls are her life, that's what her eyes tell me. Every single day she's here, walking room to room, comfortable with the sombre quiet and the sterile feel. She would never leave someone alone here, suffering on their own. But I did. She knows, and she nods curtly and steps out of my way. I don't walk through the door, though. I can't make my legs move. I just stare as it clicks shut behind her. She shakes her head one final time but says nothing as her shoes squeak their way to the next room on her list, leaving me standing in front of a closed door again.

I've opened doors in Afghan villages into rooms filled with hostiles.

I've walked into rooms with bullets flying.

I've never hesitated.

Yet here I stand, outside this room. Hesitating, with shaking hands and nothing but the same backpack I had on the plane with me. Not moving, unable to face exactly what's on the other side of that door.

My wife, and a monster I can't save her from.

2

MARK

FALL 1998

"Sorry, Laws, I'm out!" Dennis smirks over at me as he grabs the redhead's hand and heads for the bar's exit. I don't blame him; she's got great curves and she's been draped on him since five minutes after we walked in here. If I was in his shoes, I probably would have left a half hour ago, so I give him credit for sticking around this long. I can only hope he's headed to her place. Our place has thin walls.

It's been just over a year since we both got posted here after our four years at the Royal Military College, and while I love him like a brother, I'm not in any hurry to head back and risk spending the night with next-wall-over seats to the Dennis Sexytimes Show. If history is any judge, I'll be more than privy to how satisfied she'll be by morning. It's been a little too long since I've been in his shoes. Exercises, training, it feels like I'm never home and when I am, I'm exhausted. I had intended to spend tonight blowing off some steam. We just got home after two months training in Wainwright and we have nowhere else to be for a while. Once it was clear Dennis would hook up, however, I just wasn't feeling any of my options. Lately, it's all seemed like more effort than it's worth. I can't remember the last time I was with a girl that held my interest for more than one night. At only twenty-five, I think I'm losing my game. I need to get out more, with people who don't call me Lieutenant.

It's after midnight already though, and I have nowhere else to be. I decide to just head to the bathroom and then get in a cab. I haven't had enough to drink to make this bar appealing. The smell of smoke is stifling, and I cringe at the way my shoes pull up off the sticky floors with every step. This place is a cliché Army bar, complete with the young soldiers hoping to hook up with their bad haircuts and their dog tags hanging out of their shirts, and barely dressed women who can size them up and recite their base income just by looking at them. It would be funny if it wasn't also a little sad. Either way, I'm not nearly drunk enough to want to be here right now.

I pause for a moment in the hallway, debating if my bladder can wait until I get home or needs to take the chance of interrupting what's very likely to be at least some action happening in the bathroom this late into a Saturday night. The door directly in front of me flies open and I find myself with a woman in my arms.

I notice her hair first, probably because it's right in my face. It's blonde, almost white, and so fine a few pieces lift to my nose with my first intake of breath. She smells fresh and clean, and it's a welcome change from the stale smoke of the bar. I resist the urge to bury my face in it, but I do realize my hands have instinctively already come up and held onto her hips. She must be tall to come up this far on my six-foot frame, and she's curvy. My fingers sink into generous hips under what I guess is a very thin summer dress, though so far, I've only felt it. I'm sure it's only been seconds since she ran into me, but it feels far longer. I think she might feel time shift, too, as she looks up at me without backing up.

Her face is flushed, probably a little from the heat of the bar and a little from the embarrassment of the moment. Her eyes are blue, so muted they're almost grey, and the remnants of what was likely dark nightclub makeup is smudged below them. She's a natural blonde. Whatever she uses to make her eyelashes and eyebrows stand out is all but gone and the light above us makes that same white-blonde colour shimmer against her pale skin. Her face is heart shaped and her lips are a gorgeous soft pink. She's stunning, and I'm so distracted by her it takes me a moment before I realize she looks like she has been crying.

That's when the ugly lights turn on and snap us both out of it for a moment. If I thought it was the dark smoky room that made her look like that, the lights assure me that's not it. If anything, she's the only person I've ever seen that looks even better under the harsh fluorescent glow. It must be later than I thought. I glance around quickly and realize there's almost no one left that I can see, just a few groups heading towards the doors, and the music's been turned right down, making the quiet sound almost louder in its absence.

The blonde blinks once then steps back. She drops her gaze and I hear her mumbling an apology, but I find myself holding her hip a little more firmly, keeping her close to me. Her expression changes.

"Um… sorry about that. I'll just…" She tries to turn away again and thankfully, this time I find my voice instead of just holding onto her like a creeper.

"Hey. It's all right. You can bump into me anytime you want. Are you okay?"

The blonde opens her mouth then seems to change her mind about whatever she was going to say, and she closes it again. She doesn't try to move away, though, just looks at me for a moment before she decides how to answer.

"You know what? No. Not really."

"Well, I can't just let you go if you're not okay, can I? Anything I can do?" She smiles softly, a bitter-sounding laugh barely sneaks past her lips before she responds.

"Well, I came here with my friend and her boyfriend. They had brought someone for me, a blind date I guess. Then they left me here with him. Only, turns out I wasn't his… type." Her lip curls at the word *type* and her eyes shimmer. I take a moment to purposefully look her over, at least all of her that I can see when she's only six inches in front of me, making sure she understands I'm more than impressed before I answer.

"Now how do you know that? I have a hard time believing *you* wouldn't be anyone's type. Maybe he was just shy."

This time she does laugh, and shakes her head. "I don't think that was the problem." Then she gestures to a couple over by the door. The guy's not very big, probably around her height, and scrawny with a high and tight haircut and jeans that give me the impression he bought them sometime in the late eighties. His t-shirt sleeve hangs loose from his skinny arm propped up on the wall next to the head of a rail-thin brunette with too much makeup and a pair of shorts that leave very little to the imagination. If this is the girl he's ditched her for, he's more than downgraded in my opinion. It looks like he's striking out, though; the brunette shakes her head at him and ducks under his arm and out the door in one quick motion. He slowly turns around to face the bar again and I see an uncertain look on his weasely face for just a moment before he plasters on a predatory gaze when he sees the mystery blonde who still has my hand on her hip. I don't let go; if anything, I hold a little tighter and she leans in just a touch closer as he saunters over.

"Well, there you are, Megan. Looks like I'm still free tonight, so let's get out of here."

Megan. That's my blonde's name.

My blonde.

My Megan.

I might be getting ahead of myself.

I don't care.

I don't like the way this jackoff is treating her like a consolation prize after he clearly ditched her on their date to make a play for the brunette.

Megan stiffens beside me and pulls away from him as he goes to take her hand. He acknowledges me for the first time.

"Hey, man, you can't blame me for taking a shot at a girl like that!" He gestures over to where the skinny brunette ditched him. "Didn't work out, though. No harm done. This one came with me, though, so I might as well take her home. Night won't be a *total* bust."

He goes to reach for her again, but this time she steps right into me and I let her, my arm snaking all the way around her waist. The fact I just learned her name, or she doesn't even know mine yet, seems irrelevant. I pull her closer. I love the way she melts into me.

"Too late, man." I try to keep my voice calm, annoyed this guy is the distraction keeping me from finding somewhere to get to know this mystery woman better. "I don't think she's interested in going anywhere with you anymore. If she ever was."

His eyes bounce between her and me for a minute, probably weighing his options. I could save him the trouble and just tell him it won't go in his favour, but I think I'd enjoy putting this runt down. He eventually speaks up.

"Whatever. I don't need to get laid bad enough to fight off some chubby chaser. You can have her."

He's laid out on the ground, blood spurting out of his nose, before my brain even catches up with my fist. Megan beside me makes a little squeal noise and when I look over at her, her eyes are huge but they're also twinkling. I barely hear the bouncer in the distance when she grabs my hand.

"C'mon!"

She pulls me down the hall and out the emergency exit. The chill in the air of the late-night alley is exactly what I need to snap me out of my rage. I drag her around a corner, flagging a cab parked a few feet away and all but throw her inside before I jump in behind her and shut the door. I look over at her and I'm relieved to see she's not freaked out. In fact, she's full-on laughing now. Her full lips pull into the most gorgeous smile I've ever seen, her eyes dancing. The top of her strappy dress barely holds her breasts in as she shakes with laughter.

I've always been a boob guy. And those...

I shake my head. What is with this girl? I could stare at her for hours.

Her hand comes up and brushes across mine, placed on her knee. I seem to keep touching her without thinking. Her nails are perfect ovals, the blunt white tips contrasted against the rough, reddening skin of my knuckles.

I keep losing focus. We need to get out of here. I look up at her and grin.

"So... where do we go from here?"

3

MEGAN

FALL 1998

I am in a cab with the hottest man I've ever laid eyes on, and he just punched out my blind date.

I look over at where my fingers brush the cracked knuckles of his hand. Even with the redness and swelling, his hands look strong, so much bigger than mine. I've never been a small girl. Even when I was a kid, I was always bigger than all the other girls, and most of the boys, too. So, I love how he seems like such a huge presence in the car next to me. I feel like I could disappear under him.

Hell, I'm five minutes into knowing him and I already picture myself under him. I don't even know his *name*.

I need a minute.

I see him lean over to the cab driver and say something. I'm glad he has his head on. I probably would have sat here forever before I thought about telling the driver where I needed to be. When he turns back, his sparkling blue eyes smile at me.

"It's Megan, right? Hey, Megan. I'm Mark."

I just gawk for a minute and I see a question on his face for a second before he takes his hand from my knee and I instantly miss the warmth. He grabs something from his back pocket, his wallet. Flipping it open, he slides out a card and hands it to me.

It's an identification card. Not one I've seen before, and it says Canadian Forces on the top.

The guy in the picture doesn't look much like the one in front of me. He's younger, I think, and his face is drawn and serious. He has what I'm assuming is his uniform on. He looks crisp and put together. Like a cardboard cut-out.

"Mark Anthony Lawson," I manage to croak out before looking back up at him as he smiles at me. I hand him back the ID and he takes it and tucks it back away.

"That's right. I figure a woman has the right to trust the man she's with is who he says he is before she spends the night getting to know him."

I sputter, "Is that what I'm doing?"

"If you'll agree, then I'd like that. I told the driver to take us somewhere where I know we can grab a snack and then maybe take a walk. But I can have him drop you off at home if you'd rather. Or even drop me off first so I don't see where you live."

Now it's not just his eyes smiling at me, and I laugh.

"I figure a walk is the least I can do for my hero tonight."

"Trust me, Megan, getting to put down that asshole was more than its own reward."

We keep chatting as our driver winds his way through downtown and brings us in front of a Macs store. Mark hands him some cash and we step out into the dirty parking lot.

"I know what you're thinking. I'm just trying to impress you by taking you somewhere swanky."

I just shake my head and laugh as he grabs my hand and pulls me inside. He tells me he must make a quick pit stop in the bathroom and just laughs at my look of disgust that he'd use a toilet in a convenience store. I guess it's not the worst place he's ever had to go. It gives me a second to catch my breath, though, while he's gone. What the hell am I doing? This isn't like me. I don't have one-night stands, if that's even what this is. I mean, I don't have experience but I'm pretty sure most don't start with a trip for penny candies.

I've barely wrapped my head around what's happening when he's back beside me again. Soon, we make Slushies out of a dozen different flavours and bag candy from the little bins while we giggle our way around the store. The lone employee doesn't seem fazed to see grown adults acting like five-year-old kids at two in the morning, but I imagine that isn't that unusual around here.

Soon, we're back out in the still warm air of early fall and Mark has us turn off onto a walking trail that winds down the back of the neighbourhood. With mouthfuls of fuzzy peaches and sour soothers, we answer each other's questions about where we're from and what we do.

"Well, I grew up in Abbottsford. My parents were both university professors, and they didn't think they could have kids. They had a pretty quiet life, well off and a lot of travel, and then BOOM. I show up after they've been married almost twenty years. Ha! So, I was more than a little spoiled. They were so surprised when I decided to go to RMC instead of using the money they'd saved for me to go to a regular university, or even take the free tuition I could have had at the school they taught at. I'd always wanted to be a soldier, though, I guess it was too much GI Joe when I was a kid. When I left for Kingston, I don't even think they knew if they were hurt or proud."

"At least you ended up close by, hey? Do you visit them much?"

"They both died in a car accident when I was in my first year at school."

He says the words like I'm sure he has a thousand times.

Matter of fact, without much emotion. There's a silence between us, but it's not entirely uncomfortable.

"My mom died when I was eighteen, too. Breast cancer."

We're both quiet for a while. There's a comfort in someone who knows what it's like to lose a parent before their time.

There's already glimmers of light on the horizon when we finally finish talking and we're standing at the entrance of the trail where it leads out into a community.

"So, I could call you a cab…" he says as we stand staring at each other.

"Or?" I smile.

"Well, or that's my place, right over there." He points sheepishly to a small bungalow a few houses away. I burst out laughing.

"Well, isn't that *convenient*!"

"I swear, I wasn't thinking about anything except the walking trail when I had the cab bring us here…" He rubs the back of his neck with his hand and the sudden nerves are entirely out of place on the confident man I've been with up until now. I watch the muscles of his forearms bunch as he squeezes his neck and I take the moment while he's looking down to appreciate the way his shirt accents his chest, and the soft cut of his jaw and cheekbones. I feel a warm excitement I haven't felt in what seems like forever building as my eyes continue to trace down. It's evident I'm not the only one feeling it.

Mhmm, I'd disappear *right* under him.

"Well, if you're offering, soldier, I'd love to see your place."

I don't even know how we got inside. One second I'm envisioning what he'd look like without his shirt obstructing my view, the next I'm up against the cool wall in his front hallway, his body firmly but gently pinning me as his mouth finds mine. My entire body shivers at his touch, and his tongue only just barely brushes the seam of my lips when I all too happily let him in.

His hand slowly moves up my side. For some reason, his soft moan of pleasure when his hands sweep across the peak of my breast is even more sexy when his mouth is on mine, the sound caught between us.

When he breaks contact, there's a tiny squeak noise that I'm more than a little embarrassed to realize came from me. His eyes find mine, searching.

"Can I take that little disappointed noise to mean you're okay with where we're going here, babe?"

"Yes. Please." I sound breathless and a little more desperate than I intended to.

He grins, the self-assured cockiness from the bar is back, and this time when he kisses me, he presses his hips firmly into my stomach. Before I really register what's happening, my legs are wrapped around him and he's walking down the hall.

"Mark! I'm too heavy for this!" I can't remember the last time I was picked up by someone. He just chuckles into my hair.

"Doesn't look like that's true, doll."

Normally, I'd be a little offended by the nicknames, and concerned they masked an inability to remember my actual name. But he'd already moved to calling me Meg earlier in the evening. I knew that wasn't the case, and from his mouth, they sound... sexy. So, I let it slide.

We walk until I feel the softness of his bed under me. His arms place me down gently and slide their way down to the hem of my dress.

"I'm gonna need this to come off."

I briefly think of the underwear I put on this evening, a pair much more designed to hold me in than to look pretty, since I didn't envision my blind date ending this way. I wince when I look to his face as he peels the dress up, but the desire in his eyes doesn't change. It only grows. His eyes meet mine.

"Gorgeous," he growls, his lip in his teeth. "We still good, babe?"

"So, so good." I can't help my hips from rising as his hands slide my very practical control tops down my thighs. I don't have time to dwell on how embarrassing that is because it's only a moment before I feel the heat of his breath right where I want him the most.

By the time his arms are around me and I fade into sleep over an hour later, I've already decided this is the only place I ever want to be.

4

MEGAN

FALL 1998

*T*he bathroom stall at work probably wasn't the right place to do this, but I've never been patient and as soon as the thought crossed my mind, I had to know. That's how I've found myself sitting in here, staring at a tiny piece of plastic that holds my entire future in the balance. I should have had more patience and done this at home.

Now that I think of it, a little patience three weeks ago might have kept us out of this whole mess in the first place. Patience might have stopped me from immediately jumping into bed with the unreasonably hot soldier I met at a bar that night.

Okay, maybe not immediately. I mean, we did go for that walk...

Patience might have helped us wait until we had time to head to the drugstore, instead of deciding that pulling out and hoping for the best was a reasonable answer to our immediate desire.

Anyone who watched a single episode of Degrassi knows that never, ever works.

No matter how perfect the moment, or his body, seems at the time.

So here I am, surrounded by putrid peach-coloured walls in this tiny bathroom stall with my pants still around my calves, not even surprised when the first hints of that second line start to show.

Of course, I'm pregnant. In the five years since I lost my virginity in the back of Steve Densen's Dodge Neon the week before high school graduation, I've had two other partners who were both part of two long-term relationships and never even once had a scare.

But three weeks after I decide for the very first time to hook up with a guy I just met that night, and I'm officially going to be a twenty-three-year-old single mother. The man must have super sperm. Just my luck.

The truth is I've never met someone like him. The most gorgeous man I've ever seen. When he'd held onto me that first night in the bar, I couldn't believe someone like him would stand up for me, before he even knew my name. We stayed out that night talking and laughing until the early morning before making our way back to his place and not leaving until we both had to work on Monday.

I knew it had been an Army bar, but I had never dated a soldier before Mark. I'd never even considered it. Erika had convinced me to go with her and her then boyfriend Shaun and Shaun's douchebag friend Jeff. I was reluctant, but to be honest, I'd been completely focused on establishing myself into a career after college, I hadn't had a date in almost a year, so I eventually agreed. She's apologized to me a thousand times since then, but really, that awful date was the best thing that could have happened to me. Without him, I never would have found myself dragging an adrenaline-happy Mark out the fire exit after last call.

We've spent every moment we could together since then. I've never been this happy. My desire to be with him, to spend time with him, it's only gotten stronger as the days have passed. We seem to click, and as far as I can tell, he thinks so too. This, though, this wasn't part of any plan. I have no idea what he's going to think. It's one thing to be into the girl you just met. It's another thing entirely to plan a family together.

I pull up my pants, wash my hands, and walk back to my desk in a daze. I stare at my computer for the next hour, but there's no chance I'm getting any work done. Not now. The last thing I want to do is talk to people about their insurance needs. I give a quick knock on the frame of my supervisor's open door before I step in. She looks up and speaks before I can even ask.

"You look like shit. I've been telling you that all week. Go home."

I've known Erika since I started working here almost two years ago and in that time, she's become one of my closest friends, even after making me meet the asshat at the bar. She just dumped the boyfriend after and assured me I made the right call. She's one of the best people I know and completely unable to sugar coat anything. That's one of my favourite things about her.

"Thanks, Erika. I'll give you a call tonight and let you know if I'll be in tomorrow."

She disagrees, and sends me off with orders to stay in bed and drink water and not come back until Monday. As though a little rest and fluids will help me feel better.

Pretty sure that won't fix my current condition. I'll take the time, however, and hopefully before then, I'll figure out what the hell I'm going to do.

* * *

THAT PATIENCE I'm lacking probably would have helped me come up with a proper way to tell him. The logical response would be to take a few days and think it over. Come up with a plan, wait until I know what I think, what I want. I don't do that, though. I go out for a late lunch, pick at my food, talk myself through it a time or two, and then head to his place.

I've never really had a concrete plan for myself, only what I *didn't* want. I grew up in a small town where my dad worked at the jail and my mom stayed home. For my sister and me, it was expected we'd find a job that could support us until we found a man and did the same as she did. Except when I was eighteen and I watched her waste away to breast cancer, I decided as much as I loved her, I had never wanted to follow in her footsteps. She was a great mom, but by the time she died, she had done nothing for herself, never left the town she grew up in, never really lived. I decided once she was gone, I wanted to get out of town, live in the city, maybe get a cat, meet people, travel around, and explore the world. So, I went to college, got a diploma in insurance, and stayed in the city, sharing a place with my sister Cheryl and enjoying our independence. Until she decided to up and get married at twenty-one. I love Paul, I really do, and I love that I became an auntie only a year later. Now, it's just me in an apartment by myself, working so much I've never taken a real vacation, and still trying to figure out what it was I thought I was running *to* when I left home.

I can say with absolute certainty, though, I was never running to an unplanned pregnancy with a virtual stranger. I was supposed to travel the world and I've never even left Alberta. No, this is exactly the opposite of what I wanted, no matter how much he makes my heart melt.

I decided there's no reasonable way you tell a man you met three weeks ago that you're carrying his child. I briefly consider not saying anything to him at all and figuring it out on my own. Calling Cheryl instead and planning over chocolate. Her daughter Layne is only fourteen months, our kids could grow up together. I'm sure I could be a single mom. I have a good job, benefits. Plenty of women go that route and do it well.

If I did that, however, I'd have to stop seeing him. There's no way I could keep it a secret while still hanging out with him almost every day. Every time I think of that, it physically hurts. I don't believe in love at first sight, or even love at three weeks. There's no way I could be in love yet. I can't explain it, though. I've never felt quite so attached to anyone before, and I can't imagine walking away. For better or worse, I guess now we're in this together.

At least I hope we are. Do I really know him well enough to think he won't run? There's no way I can guarantee he'll stick this out. I must give him the option, though. Even if his answer might gut me.

So here I am. Sitting on his front step, my ass slowly cooling at the feel of the concrete.

I see his car pull up; he backs in his spot and gets out, grabbing his backpack from the backseat before he walks up. He's still in his uniform, the faded green is almost worn through in places and looks even worse next to the relative new fabric of his backpack. It still does something to me, though. I never pictured myself with a soldier. I barely understood what the military did when I met him. He's tried to explain, tried to tell me what an infantry officer does. I figure I understand it about as well as he understands insurance underwriting. There's still something about a man in uniform, though.

The shiny metal badge on his beret catches the afternoon sun. With that beret on, I can't see that he has any hair at all, even though I know when he takes it off, he has a shock of almost-too-long straight brown hair underneath. His eyes are a gentle brown, framed by lashes any woman would be envious of. Especially a woman like me whose own are too light to be seen. He has a strong jaw and broad shoulders. The way he walks is confident and purposeful. That's one of my favourite things about him. The way he moves, the way he takes over a room just by being in it, the way he makes me feel like, even when we're running from bouncers in the early hours of the morning, he's always completely in control. He gives me goosebumps every single time I see him, and when he notices me sitting here and quickens his step, bounding up to me with a grin on his face, my heart leaps and for just one moment, I forget why I'm here.

Just a moment, though.

"Hey, Meg, I wasn't expecting…"

"I'm pregnant."

My words hang in the air between us, but his smile doesn't falter. He stops a foot from me and cocks his head to the side.

"Huh. Well, all right then."

His eyes don't leave mine. His complete refusal to immediately panic must be the single-most frustrating thing he's ever done.

"All right? ALL RIGHT? That's all you're going to say?"

"What do you want me to say, Meg? We slept together. A lot. We didn't always do it the safest way we could. I took sex ed. I can't say I didn't know this was a possibility."

He pulls out the right key and he unlocks the front door. I stand on the step, still staring at him as he walks inside. Looking back at me, he takes a long look at my face and very deliberately puts his bag down, pulling me into himself and wrapping his arms tightly around me for a moment before grabbing my hand, and dragging me inside.

"Mark! This isn't me telling you I want to order Chinese or even that I bought a puppy. I'm. Pregnant. I AM HAVING A BABY."

He puts his bag on the chair by the door and his keys on the kitchen counter, then turns to look at me again.

"Okay."

"WHAT IS WRONG WITH YOU?"

Mark chuckles and suddenly, my feet are out from under me and he's carrying me over to the couch before he sets me down and kneels between my knees, looking up at me.

I am not a small woman, by any estimation, and every time he scoops me up off my feet, it catches me off guard.

"I'm sorry. I'm not sure the right answer here. This is the first time anyone's ever told me they're pregnant with my baby and... It *is* my baby, right? Is there any chance it's not?"

His voice is kind when he asks, but it's like his question breaks the frayed thread that had been holding my sanity together these past few hours since I took the test. I immediately cry.

"Yes, it's yours! Why else would I be here, Mark? Why else would I come here? Do you think I planned this?"

"I don't know, Megan! I don't know what answer you want from me!"

Now I'm sobbing. Thick tears down my face and over my hands. Ugly, choking noises from my mouth. My nose starts running and my shoulders shake. I don't even realize Mark has moved until I feel his arms entirely around me, covering me, like he's enveloping me into himself.

"I'm sorry. I'm sorry, I'm saying all the wrong things apparently. So how about I just shut up and let you talk, yeah? Whenever you're ready. I'm listening, I'm not going anywhere."

It takes me a long time to be ready. I stop crying but I'm still quiet and I sit there in his arms, just drawing strength from his body around me. Even now, even with this looming disaster, he makes me feel calmer, happier. He makes it... Easier. Better.

I don't like how much I already need him.

This isn't the independence I thought I wanted.

When I think I can talk without dissolving again, I look up at him.

His beret is off, his hair a slightly sweaty mess sticking up on his head. His lips are turned up slightly, almost hopeful. His eyes search mine, his expression open, kind, compassionate. Loving.

Oh God, I hope I'm not imagining that part. I need that to be real. For both of us. For all *three* of us.

"I'm sorry. I've never done this before either." We both smile a little now. The skin on my cheeks is tight as my tears dry and he raises a hand to my face and brushes back the hair that's stuck there.

"Let's start over. Okay. I'll try again." I swallow, take a deep breath, and make a fresh start.

"Mark, I took a test this morning and it says I'm pregnant. We're having a baby. I didn't plan this, and I know you didn't either, but it happened and since I haven't been with anyone else in over a year, there's no doubt you are the father.

"So... where do you want to go from here?"

5

MARK

PRESENT

*T*he chair in this room is only big enough for about half of me.

I find myself shifting around for the five hundredth time as I watch the same judgemental nurse as before while she looks at all the monitors in the room and writes things on her notepad before she silently slips out the door, not even acknowledging me. The doctor left just before her. He said a lot of words, all of them hurt.

None of them more than the first question.

"How did you not know?"

She's so pale, the white tape holding the IV line in her hand is almost indistinguishable against her skin. Her chest rises and falls so slightly I find myself pressing my hand on her, so I can feel it move under me. Her collarbone is pronounced. I rub my thumb along it as it seems to jut out from her skin unnaturally. Did it look like that before I left?

"How did you not know?"

She had lost some weight. I remember that. But she was always trying to lose weight. That wasn't a red flag. Was there one?

She had been tired, but that was nothing new. She was parenting two kids on her own most of the time. Add going back to work on top of that and I just assumed she was keeping herself busy. I mean, isn't everyone tired?

"How did you not know?"

I reach out and brush the hair from where it's stuck to her lip. Those fine streaks of darker blonde, lowlights she called them, have grown almost halfway down the length of her strands. She always kept up with things like that. When was the last time she'd had her hair done?

"How did you not know?"

The last thing the doctor told me before he left me in here with her was that she's not sedated. She's on some heavy-duty painkillers and antibiotics, but she *could* wake up. Nothing is keeping her unconscious. Her body is just so physically exhausted she stays sleeping. He said, despite her treatments and illness and all the warnings to take it easy, she had quite literally pushed herself until her body gave out from under her. She has nothing left now. Not even enough in her to open her eyes.

"How did you not know?"

I think back to the first few weeks after I met Megan. I fell so fast, it was all such a whirlwind. We spent every moment we could manage in each other's arms. I felt like I had memorized every single inch of her skin, every freckle, every crease, every curve. The way my fingers fit in the dimples at the small of her back. The weight of her breasts in my hands. The feel of her lips on my neck. The feather-soft skin right behind her ear. I used to tell her how beautiful she was like it was my mantra, repeating it whenever I saw her, each time I felt her skin under mine.

Those days when I closed my eyes, I could see every detail of her clear as day in my mind.

Now I look at her and I can't remember if I knew she had taken out that tragus piercing she used to have in her left ear. How long she's had those dark circles etched under her eyes. It looks like she must have had her eyelashes and eyebrows tinted since they're darker now even when her face is obviously bare of any makeup. I can't remember when I stopped telling her how much I loved the look of her blonde hair, or when the last time I reminded her how the light colour of her eyelashes made it look like there was a soft glow around her eyes in the light.

I leave my fingertips on her skin, running them all the way down her neck and shoulders until I reach her hands.

A few of her nails have ragged edges and the soft blue polish is chipped.

Her nail polish is never chipped. My hand shakes as I hold on to hers.

I can't let her nails stay this way. She'd hate this. Why didn't they have someone come in and fix them?

I find myself wondering if there's a travelling salon I could hire to fix up her nails for her.

I'm still on that ridiculous thought, staring at her hand in mine, when I hear her voice

"Mark? What are you doing here?"

6

MARK

WINTER 1999

*I*t should not take this much effort to move your pregnant girlfriend in with you.

I feel like it's just common sense. We're having a baby. How does she think this is going to work? We'll what, keep two places and move back and forth? She'll move the baby in with her and I can come visit?

I don't fucking think so.

Right now, Megan is getting ready in the bathroom at my place, so we can meet her sister and brother-in-law for dinner. They have some baby things for her, though I don't know why they're getting rid of anything since they seem to pop the things out like rabbits. But who am I to refuse a head start on the apparently ten thousand things we need to get for the baby?

"Meg, we're going to be late!"

She pokes her head out of the bathroom, half her blonde hair falling gracefully and curled under her chin. The other half seems to have been caught in a freak rainstorm.

"For the five hundredth time, on time isn't late."

I loudly plop myself down on the couch. Yes. It is. Ten minutes early is five minutes late. We've been over this. We're always late.

"We aren't always late. And it's just my sister, Mark. Relax, I'm almost done."

Shit. I didn't mean to say that part aloud.

She looks the opposite of *almost done*, but while I might be new at this, I think saying that might be the wrong idea. Instead, I turn on the TV. Loudly.

Ten minutes later, she emerges and this time her hair matches on both sides. She's wearing a long stretchy dress that outlines the extra bump she's just started to show in front of her. She's always been the most beautiful woman I've ever seen, but that bump, knowing it's my child in there, makes her impossibly perfect.

I stand quickly in front of her, my hands alternating between her belly and her already more than generous breasts that now spill out of everything. She hates it. I, on the other hand, am not complaining. At. All.

"Mark! You were JUST complaining we were going to be late. Honestly."

She tries to skirt by me, so I give her ass a good smack on the way by for good measure. It takes me about double the time it should to get my shoes on since she's bent over struggling with hers and the view is spectacular.

"You know, you could give me a hand…"

"Yup. I probably could."

"Pervert."

We're fifteen minutes late to the restaurant but Megan insists that's still on time. I swear she does this just to annoy me. Cheryl and Paul are just getting seated, though, so we head over to join them, and they're soon lost in talks of birth, breastmilk, and whatever the hell a bassinet is.

Apparently, we absolutely need one.

Eventually, I tune them both out and Paul and I move on to different topics.

At first, I didn't think I'd like the guy, but he's grown on me. I had assumed just by looking at him, with his tall but lean shape, dark-rimmed glasses, perpetually messy black hair, and stupid goatee, that he'd be a flake. I have to say, though, for a man with a house as loud as his and a wife who seems hell bent on driving him completely up the wall, he's one of the most laid-back guys I know.

We talk about hockey for a while, and the new F150. Local politics.

"That's quite the mess up there in Europe, ain't it?"

This time I freeze, glancing over at Megan. Thankfully, Paul takes the hint and shifts the topic to basement renos, but not without a look telling me we're going to discuss this later. When the girls excuse themselves to the bathroom while we wait for the bill, he wastes no time, either.

"So, what the hell?"

"I don't know anything, man. It's just looking like, you know, it might possibly be something. But who knows, shit like this happens all the time. We haven't been told anything. It could all blow into nothing."

"Or it might not. You have a pregnant girlfriend, Mark. Have you warned her?"

"No. And I'm not going to and neither are you. It's probably nothing and I'm having a hard-enough time convincing her to move in with me as it is. She won't even consider getting married. I know, because I keep asking. It's a delicate fucking balance here. I tell her I might be leaving, and she'll bolt."

"You're not giving her enough credit."

"Oh ya, then why won't she marry me, hey? We're having a kid. Yet it's still taking me everything just to get her to live in the same house with me. I have a six-week exercise coming up where I won't be home and she's already asked me ten thousand questions about how this works. I'm having a hard-enough time trusting she'll even wait that long. I need her connected to me with more than a smile and a handshake before I start throwing deployments around. I'm not risking it."

I hear the girls giggling behind me and the conversation ends, but not before Paul shakes his head at me sadly.

I'm doing the right thing here.

I think.

7

MEGAN

SPRING 1999

"Where is the damn anesthesiologist?"

I swear Mark is about ready to lose his mind and we just got here. For an entirely calm guy, he is about ready to take down the whole maternity ward.

The doctor between my legs who has his fingers somewhere near my ovaries if I could guess by how it feels, pulls them out and sits back.

"Sorry to be the bearer of bad news, folks, but you're already at eight-centimetres dilation. We're not going to have time to get an epidural in, I'm afraid. There are other options, however..."

"WHAT DO YOU MEAN SHE CAN'T HAVE AN EPIDURAL?" Mark bellows and the doctor steps back a few inches. I squeeze his hand.

"Let him tell me what I *can* have, Mark!"

The doctor proceeds to tell me all about the various painkilling options and in a few minutes, I have a shot of morphine and some gas at my disposal to take the edge off. Mark still paces by the bed, he doesn't sit until the drugs kick in and I catch my breath. He brushes the hair off my face and his worried eyes drill into me.

"I hate this."

I let out a small laugh. He hates this? It's not exactly a picnic on my end, either.

"Women do it every day," I tell him. "I, however, am never, ever doing it again." I squeeze his hand harder as another contraction hits. He's been my rock through this entire pregnancy. The ultrasounds and the tests, the morning sickness and the swollen ankles. I somewhat reluctantly moved in with him this spring before he had to head out for a couple months for work. I had been putting it off, unwilling to let go of that last bit of independence. He convinced me by saying he wanted me to have access to everything while he was gone, but I know he had just been waiting for the right time to corner me into making the move. It only made sense. We had agreed to do this together so having a baby while living apart wouldn't really work. And he had a house he'd bought with the money from his parents, so his place was the best option. Still, giving in was harder than I thought. It wasn't that I didn't want to be with him; it was more I didn't want to give up being on my own.

When he left, I realized how much I relied on him and his time away was an eye opener for me. Adjusting to military life isn't as seamless as I thought; there's a lot more to it than I realized. The six that turned into seven weeks he was gone was the first of what I've grown to understand will be many separations, and I've never been more grateful for having my sister close by as I took my time understanding that even with him as a partner, I'd be doing a lot of this alone. I hadn't anticipated how long the nights would feel.

My things aren't even all unpacked at his place, but we have a baby room mostly set up where his old roommate used to be. I felt bad he moved out, but Mark said he was headed to Bosnia soon for six months. It ended up saving him the rent money he gave Mark anyways. We painted the room, all greens and yellows since whoever this little one in here is didn't want to sit pretty for the ultrasound tech. I can't say I even have a preference. Right now, all I care about is getting the bugger the hell out of my body.

"Whatever you say, babe."

I take a few deep breaths as the contraction pain passes and I have another minute to regroup. I look over at Mark, who has a glass of ice chips in one hand and the nitrous mask in the other. He looks almost worse off than I am.

"You're freaking me out, Mark. Stop looking at me like I'm dying!" He looks chastised, and attempts a smile.

Oh man, that is worse. I immediately regret my request.

I don't have time to think on it though, because I'm in the throes of another contraction when I hear him speak again.

"I need you to marry me, Megan. Please. Please say you'll marry me."

"Are you kidding me right now, Mark? Seriously?" I bite out once I have caught my breath. He's been asking the same thing for months. It's not that I don't want to marry him, I do. I think I fell in love with him the moment he bruised his knuckles on that useless jerk at the bar. I just don't want to marry him for the reasons he wants to marry me. We've gone over this a thousand times in the last eight months.

"C'mon, Megan. You're having my baby! It's too late now to marry you before the birth, but please, just say you will. At least then it's my fiancée having my baby. Please."

I can't answer for a moment and he's distracted holding the gas over my face and silently counting out the seconds of my contraction with the beat of his thumb on the hand I'm gripping. I don't think he even knows he's doing it. I force myself to look up at him and look in his eyes as the pain washes over and finally recedes. I can barely catch my breath though. The nurse who's sitting with what must be a stellar view of all I have to offer looks up and smiles.

"You're going to want to start pushing, Megan. This little one is right there. It's time!"

I take some deep breaths trying to calm myself. I glance back at Mark and his eyes plead. I don't know if it's about the baby or the fact I won't answer him. Probably both. I finally snap. We've gone back and forth on this for months and if he hasn't figured out why I can't agree, he never will.

"Mark, I won't marry someone who is only doing it because they have to. I can't marry someone who doesn't love me!"

I yell the last bit as the next contraction hits and he freezes. It takes one of the nurses gently reminding him I need the gas for him to remember to put the mask back on my face as I push with all I have. The silence in the room is almost comical, considering what's going on. It's just my breathing that sounds as loud as an elephant in my head, and the slow rise and fall of the blood pressure machine strapped to my arm.

Time is irrelevant for minutes. Hours. All I can think of is the pain, the next wave, the next push.

"Megan…" When I look up, I swear there are tears in his eyes.

"Megan, I can't believe I never told you… I just assumed… God, Megan, of course I love you."

I can't think. I can't think about this.

"I can feel the head. Baby is right there. One more push, Mama!" The nurse calls out and Mark breaks his eyes from me to look down as I take one more breath and give it all I have. Fuck, it hurts. It seems to go on forever before I feel the relief of the pressure leaving my body and I instantly look down just as a small, squirming, bloody mess is unceremoniously placed on my stomach.

"It's a girl!" Mark's voice is so quiet, but I can hear it clear as anything. He is back up next to me, wiping the strands of hair stuck to the sweat and tears on my cheek. "You did amazing, Megan. You *are* amazing. She's perfect. I love you so much."

I finally take a deep breath and look around the room, for the first time really comprehending how much everyone in here would have heard of our conversation that whole time. It's hard to be embarrassed, however, since most of them have also had their hands up my hoohah several times in the past four hours. They might as well be all up in my regular business, too.

He asked me to marry him.

Again.

I said no.

Again.

He said he loves me.

Wait… he loves me?

And now my daughter, my daughter is right there. Mark cuts the cord and the nurses take her to give her a checkup, weigh and measure her. My eyes don't leave her as they move her around the room.

"Does the wee princess have a name?" the nurse, a loud, portly woman with vibrant red hair and a thick Scottish accent asks after giving us all the other relevant details.

Mark looks at me and I nod to him.

"Yes. Her name is Victoria. Victoria Anne Lawson."

Anne. Like my mom. It takes me back for a moment. How much I wish she was here, right now, to share this with me.

The nurse smiles and places Victoria in Mark's waiting arms. Tears fall unashamed down his face as he smiles at her. The slightly too long hair from the top of his head falls onto his forehead and I can hear the hitch in his breath. If I hadn't already fallen head over heels, I wouldn't stand a chance right now. My heart fills completely watching him with our little girl.

These last months have been more than either of us

expected. I can't deny, however, how much he has stepped up. I've had doubts, so many doubts, but he's never wavered.

"Did you mean it, Mark?"

He doesn't even look up, doesn't hesitate.

"I've never meant anything more. I'm so sorry I ever gave you reason to think I don't."

"Then my answer is yes."

This time he does look up and the happiness I see in his eyes catches my breath. He leans down and kisses me softly. I'm sure the cooling sweat and slightly metallic breath I must have from the dried blood inside my cheeks from biting down are super sexy, but he doesn't say a word. He places Victoria in my arms before he steps back.

"Thank you," he whispers. "Can we get married this month, then?"

I just stare at him blankly.

This month? That's not how weddings work. Surely, he knows that. Not to mention we literally just this moment had a baby. The man is completely insane.

"Mark, we have time…"

"That's the thing…" Suddenly, this man who has been looking me in the eye for the past four hours as I squeezed his child out can't meet my gaze.

"Mark…"

"Thing is… I got the call this morning before we left. The unit is leaving for Kosovo next month."

Fuck.

Well, I guess this is one way to learn how to be an Army wife.

* * *

APPARENTLY ONE OF the things people forgot to tell me was it takes about thirty-eight seconds after they leave for everything to go wrong.

Literally no one is surprised when it happens, though, so I know they all knew this was a thing. Would have been nice for a head's up.

Tori won't stop crying. She won't. I bounce, I sing, I do all the fancy things the parenting magazine tells me to. I get nowhere. That girl has a set of lungs on her like nothing I've ever heard and I'm pretty sure I'm losing my mind along with the silence. I haven't dressed in days. It could be a week, I'm not sure. I really, really need groceries, but I can't bring myself to bring this banshee out in public. Cheryl has been helping where she can, but she's pregnant and right now her and Layne are out with a stomach bug. It's just me and this devil spawn every single day, staring at each other.

I barely hear the doorbell, and it takes me a long time to realize what the sound is when I do. Cheryl has a key and I can't remember the last time someone rang the bell. Funny thing happens when you have a baby. Your friends who don't aren't all that interested in coming around to see you and the howling monkey all the time.

I never thought the biggest struggle of bringing another human into this world would be loneliness.

I open the door to Erika, smiling at me with two cups of Starbucks in her hands.

"Hey, Megan, can I come in? I brought chai!"

"Are you alone?" I ask only because I don't think I even know where a bra is right now.

"Sure am, love."

I open the door the rest of the way before half-heartedly moving the partially folded laundry off the couch, so we have somewhere to sit. I lift the collar of my shirt and smell myself. Thankfully, Tori seems to like bathing so I'm not too bad. I lift Tori, who's as usual plastered to my hip, up and smell her bum.

She's good too. Even if we weren't, there's no time to fix anything anyways. I don't even bother to look in the mirror.

Erika's fiery red hair is loose, down almost to her hips, and her whole face smiles when she does. Her hazel eyes warm and the freckles on her face softens her almost elvish features. She's always loved makeup and today is no exception as a warm navy blue frames her lids and her lips are a golden colour. She's in jeans and a wraparound tank top that only girls like her, with lean torsos and not an ounce of extra jiggle, can pull off.

I look down at my sweatpants and maternity t-shirt. My hair is a plastered mess on my head, I'm sure. I haven't even considered it in a long time. My figure, that hasn't fit into Erika's size since I was ten anyways, is stretched out and still holding at least half the considerable weight I gained during the pregnancy. I can only imagine what she thinks when she looks at me.

I've been on maternity leave for a couple months now. Every week, I plan to bring Tori down to visit the office, but every week, it seems like a worse and worse idea. People want to visit with a happy, cooing baby, not a red-faced siren. I haven't seen Erika since Mark left six weeks ago. Every time she calls, I brush off a visit, saying Victoria is too fussy and maybe the next week will be better. But the next week is never, ever better.

Erika puts the cups down on the counter next to me, brushing aside the cups and bottles and soothers that clutter the top, and the smell of warm chai filters into the air beside me. My favourite. I'm surprised Erika remembers, but then again, she doesn't have a tiny human demanding every brain cell she has right now.

"Oh, look at her! Meg, she's getting so big! Look how gorgeous she is, and all that hair!"

It's true, the child is growing at an alarming rate. It's to be expected, considering I'm almost five feet ten and Mark is a solid six feet. I look at her differently, now. Maybe it's because I

FIGHT FOR HOME

try to see her through someone else's eyes instead of mine, the ones that have had to listen to her cry for weeks on end. When I look at her objectively, I see her a little differently. When she's quiet, she really is beautiful.

I chastise myself for losing sight of that. What kind of mother forgets to notice how gorgeous her daughter is?

Erika puts her arms out and I gingerly place a squirming Victoria into them. Next to Erika's slender frame, she looks gigantic as Erika hops around the living room with her, cooing in her ear. I wait for the screaming to start. The screaming always starts.

The screaming doesn't start.

What the hell?

Victoria looks up at Erika like she's never seen another human being in her short little life; her eyes are wide and clear. I stand there, gaping at them.

Is she serious?

"Look at this angel. Oh, Meg, you're so lucky. She's just perfect."

I can't even form words for a moment. Is this child purposely trying to make me look like a crazy person? Does she want people to think I am completely nuts when I tell them she won't stop crying? Does she hate me? Because from the look of this, she's entirely happier with this woman she's only met once before in her life, instead of the woman who's been holding her, feeding her. and changing her around the clock for weeks.

Traitor.

I finally find my voice.

"Apparently…" Erika smiles over at me, with Tori's eyes still happily fixated on her face.

"Kids are always better for other people than they are for their parents."

"Maybe you should take her home then…" I mumble under my breath, but Erika just laughs.

39

"Oh, hun. You need a break. You look like shit and so does this place. When was the last time you showered on your own, or took a nap by yourself?"

I glance around. Erika's honesty isn't even offensive; it's not like there's any use pretending she doesn't notice the dirty dishes, laundry piles, delivery boxes, or what I'm sure is the unpleasant smell of a home that hasn't been cleaned or aired out in weeks.

I'm as much of a mess as this house is.

"Go take a shower."

"Oh, I couldn't... I mean, what if she gets hungry."

"Megan, I'm not a baby expert but I don't believe a child can starve in a half hour if you take the time to take a shower. Just go. And when you get out, lie down. Victoria and I will hang out here and watch a movie." Erika moves some more of the laundry off the bouncy chair and plops herself on the couch, setting Victoria on her lap facing her.

"I'll come get you if we need your boobs."

I keep staring blankly. I don't know if it's because of her words, because Victoria isn't crying, or because the only other adult I've seen in days has been the delivery guy, but I can't seem to process what she's saying.

"Go!"

I blink a couple times and head to the bedroom, stripping down almost robotically and running the shower in the ensuite. The bathroom floor is covered in baby towels and bath toys that are almost entirely useless for a baby who's not yet three months old. As steam drifts into the room, I step inside. It feels amazing, the actual hot water against my skin. I don't think I've had anything more than a lukewarm bath with Tori in forever. My skin turns pink from the heat, but I don't even care. I just stand there, my head bowed under the rush of hot water, and feel it hit my body and run down my back and shoulders.

I'm so tired. Every part of me is just sore from exhaustion. I lather and rinse, washing my oily hair three times before I feel myself. Once I'm clean, I still can't find my way out of the water.

It's been several days since I've heard from Mark. The last time he called, the satellite delay and static from the line was so bad I could barely hear him, and once Victoria woke up and started fussing, it was a lost cause. Late at night, when I'm delirious from lack of sleep and she's wide awake, I show her photos of him and tell her stories about how we met, even about the courthouse wedding that only Cheryl and Mark's friend Dennis attended. I let her curl up in the green t-shirt I've kept here unwashed. I silently pray she soaks in his scent, that she somehow learns to recognize it when he comes home.

Whenever that is.

I miss his heat in the bed, and the way he can make me feel covered. I miss sitting at home with a rented movie and pizza, and laughing with him. I miss my best friend.

These days though, I wonder if I don't miss the help more. I want him, but really, I want another adult in the house to hand the baby to. To hold her while I take a shower and a nap and make dinner. To understand with me the crying and to make decisions with me like when I should take her to the doctor, if the fever is important, what teething looks like, and what kind of rash means I must go to the walk-in clinic.

I miss not being the only one in charge.

If I'm honest, I miss the life I had planned, of travelling and beaches and adventure.

What kind of mother dreams of a life without kids?

What kind of wife dreams of running away when her husband is halfway across the world?

Before I even realize it, I'm sitting on the floor of the shower. My eyes are closed, my hands in front of my face so I can breathe through the steady stream of hot water that hides the tears.

8

MEGAN

PRESENT

I can hear the beeping of the machines and feel the touch on my hand before I even open my eyes. It feels like there's an elephant sitting on my chest and razor blades in my throat. I sit for a minute before opening my eyes. I know where I am. I have vague memories of collapsing in the parkade at work, the sounds of the people around me as they called the ambulance. I must be at the hospital. I'm not sure how long it's been, but I'm pretty sure it's been more than a day or two. I can remember bits and pieces: my sister coming and going, telling me she and Paul had the kids. I remember a moment awhile back when the nurse changed the IV. I don't know if that was today or yesterday. I'm a mess.

All that effort I put in, trying to avoid any of this and yet here I am. What kind of mother lets this happen, when I haven't even been caring for my own kids? What a complete failure. Before I even get my eyes open, I resolve to get my shit together and get out of here. I don't have time for this.

It takes several moments before I manage to crack my lids open. They feel like they're weighted down. I know there's someone else in the room with me and I'm hoping it's Cheryl, letting me know how the kids are doing. I don't even think I asked her last time she was in here. I can only imagine what she thinks of me. What everyone must think.

Poor Megan can't deal. She can't cope on her own, she can't hack it.

Dammit. I can, and I will!

I just need to get my eyes open and get out of this bed.

When I finally pry them a crack and let the light in, however, it all comes crashing down.

"Mark? What are you doing here?"

I don't know how long he's been here, but I startle him by speaking. He'd been looking down at where our hands are linked, and his eyes jump to mine at the sound of my voice. He looks terrible with his hair matted down on his head, his blood-shot eyes rimmed in red; the dark circles underneath them seem so heavy they're dragging his face down. I don't think I've ever seen him look this defeated. If he's had to come all the way back here just for this, I can only guess how frustrated he must be with me.

All this work and I've still failed.

He doesn't answer right away, just stares at me for a moment. I'm almost grateful for it. I can't bear to hear his disappointment. It takes me so much effort just to keep my eyes open I say nothing else and the silence between us seems to stretch on forever.

Finally, he seems to find his voice.

"Of course, I'm here, Megan." His voice is hoarse, almost as bad as mine. Of course, he's here? What's that supposed to mean? I didn't call him. I know Cheryl didn't call. Why would I assume he'd be here when I never intended him to know about it at all?

"I didn't tell anyone to call you." Every syllable hurts as it scrapes its way out of my throat.

"You should have."

His voice is firm. It's that tone I hate, the one that sounds like he's directing his troops instead of talking to his wife. It grates on me. I was doing just fine, there was no need for him to come all the way home for this. If he is going to sit here and tell me now he's decided I can't handle things without him, he can go to hell. I've been doing it our entire marriage. I can handle this, and he can worry about his job without worrying about me.

"I'm fine. You can go back, I don't need you."

His whole body recoils from me like he's been burnt. He pulls his hand back roughly, not moving his eyes off mine. For a moment, I see what looks like pain in them, but that is quickly replaced by anger and I wonder if I really saw it at all.

My eyes are throbbing; it feels like there are tiny strings pulling them closed and try as I might, I can't seem to fight them anymore. I'm just so tired.

Right as I fall into unconsciousness, I swear I hear Mark's voice.

"But I need you."

9

MARK

FALL 1999

*H*oly hell, it's been a long six months.
As I pack up my things, I find myself staring at the top of my barracks box a little too long. It's covered with the photos Megan has sent me, of Victoria as she's growing up. She's got my dark hair, growing into bouncing curls. With Megan's almost-clear blue eyes. I never realized how much love would change when I had a child of my own. I never even realized complete devotion was something I was capable of, but even having been able to hold her for such a short amount of time, she's wrapped up my whole world.

There are almost no photos of Megan. Phone calls home have been a rare luxury here, but every time I've got to hear her voice, I've asked her for photos. She just laughs me off, and sends more of Victoria in the mail. All the pictures of her I have are ones I took with me when I left. My favourite is the one of her from the hospital, her hair matted and her cheeks flushed, her forehead dotted with burst blood vessels, our newborn daughter feeding from her breast.

She's never looked more beautiful.

Some days, especially when the weeks dragged and we couldn't get to a phone for a while, I finally close my eyes at night and make myself hear her voice in my head before I fall asleep. I can't let myself forget. I won't.

At least time passes relatively quickly when you're working twelve-hour shifts and then spending the rest of your down time writing reports on those shifts. I haven't had too much time to devote to missing home, to missing my family.

Most of the time, I'm just grateful she still answers the phone when I call. I trust her, with everything, but it's hard not to let the number of Dear John letters and unanswered phone calls happening all around me get to me. I had always heard rumours of soldiers coming home to houses that had been emptied in the night, no one there to greet them when they land. I always thought they were exaggerations, stories told how soldiers do of things that they heard from a friend of a friend, always made bigger than it was. But so far, I've seen at least a half-dozen men break down when letters came in or when phone calls show a line has been disconnected. It's hard to believe there's anyone willing to wait, even as Megan keeps answering the phone.

Danger has been low here, but tensions are high. Some of the things we've all seen have only been made worse by how little we can do about it. It seems for every arrest we can make, every attack we can prevent on one innocent, it's only a drop in the ocean compared to the atrocities going on all around us.

We aren't the ones in danger, the civilians here are. Sometimes from their own authorities.

That's not how it's supposed to work. I'd so much rather be the one who must fight. Instead, the biggest threat I've faced was pneumonia. I can't shoot pneumonia, and worse, I couldn't get my men the equipment they needed to defend against it, either.

As a leader, I feel useless. My men got sick while the women and children around us live in a fear we can't properly defend them from. Not when the rules barely let us defend ourselves.

"Hey, Laws!" Dennis calls me out of my own head.

"You got the last patrol report done?"

I look over at my friend standing at the entrance of our mod tent. His face is grizzled in a now perpetual sunburn, even after the weather got cold here. I think he was just already so burnt his skin will never stop being a little red, the shade making his olive skin look almost leather like. It makes his whole face look older, especially with the day's growth on his cheeks. His hair has long since moved past regulation length; so far no one here gives a shit. He just keeps pushing to see how far he can go with it. The top now grazes his eyebrows in a matted brown wave.

He plops down heavy on the cot next to me, his eyes sweeping the photos that are curling up at the edges.

"You must be stoked to get to see her soon, eh?"

His eyes don't hold the enthusiasm of his voice. They were always dark but lately, they look black and cold. He is already struggling with the feeling of helplessness being here and knowing the horror that is happening when there is so little he can do. Dennis has always been loud, abrasive, but soft inside. He needs to help, he needs to fix, and here… well, here he can't. I watched it break his spirit all tour.

Then last month on a routine patrol where they had a couple humanitarian workers with them, they only barely managed to stop one of the female aid workers from being raped by an off-duty Russian soldier. Even once they got to her, the most they could do was have him and the men with him arrested and handed over to the corrupt local authorities. Chances are it was laughed off. I wouldn't be surprised if he was already back at work.

I wish I could say it was an isolated incident, but we've been hearing similar stories of threats and danger to aid workers and interpreters every week. The line between authority and bad guy has been long crossed here. It's frustrating as hell to stand and see the corruption.

His anger over it all was justified, but when the aid worker disappeared on a flight out shortly after without saying a word, his hurt spoke to more. I think he had felt something for her; maybe they even skirted the radar together as a couple. I haven't asked, and I probably should have, but everyone can see how much it broke him down.

"Ya, man, I'm pretty stoked. Victoria is almost eight months old. She's growing so fast. What about you, what are you going to do when you get home?"

He looks at me with a grin that is more predatory than happy.

"I'm going to sleep in my own comfortable bed for a fucking week. Then I'm going to grab some Jack and Coke, and the closest willing woman, and I'll lock myself in until I have to get back to work."

"You know, once you're tired of booze and pussy, you always have a spot at our table, hey?"

"No chance of that happening!!"

I just shake my head at him and grab my gear to head out the door. He stays still a moment.

"But, you know, thanks, man."

I bump his shoulder on the way out.

"Of course."

I can't wait to get the hell out of here, and I've never been more grateful to have my woman back home waiting.

10

MEGAN

SPRING 2000

I've never both simultaneously loved and hated someone quite as much as I have Mark these past six months.

I thought... I thought the deployment was the hard part.

It was hard, don't get me wrong. So, so hard.

This last bit, however, is no walk in the park either.

I guess we can chalk that up to one more thing no one warned me about. Though, these days, it feels more and more like maybe no one told us because we're the only ones it's happening to.

I mean, when they get back, it's supposed to be the easy part. He's the love of my life, the father of my baby girl. He's who I was pining after, who I was missing for half of a year.

Then he came home.

It was beautiful, that moment when I saw him at the training hall when he got off the bus. Victoria and I had been waiting there for hours and let me tell you, keeping an overtired seven-month-old amused in a giant, crowded, hot gymnasium isn't even as easy as it sounds. And it sounds terrible.

I mostly made myself feel better by reminding myself that I could be the woman by herself in the corner who I'm almost positive had nothing on underneath the long black overcoat she wore.

I had to admire her boldness, but I didn't envy the sweat.

By the time he finally walked in, Tori was D.O.N.E. To be completely honest, so was I. There couldn't have been much left of the makeup I had painstakingly applied four hours earlier, and that subtle yet difficult curl I'd perfected in my hair had given way to a sweaty, flat mess.

It all faded, though, when his eyes met mine. His bag fell beside him, and he crushed me to him, trapping a squealing Victoria in the middle. It's like my whole body melted, the feeling of relief with his arms around me again, knowing he's home. There's no other feeling that can come close to that first embrace after a deployment is over.

We clung to each other that night. I thought he would fall asleep standing up and I was sure once we had Victoria settled in bed, he'd be out. Instead, he studied every inch of me. It was like he'd never seen me before and he couldn't get enough. I don't think I've ever felt as desirable as I did that night under my insatiable soldier. It was like he felt like he had to re-imprint himself on my skin.

That fairytale, though, it didn't last. Not even through the week.

Victoria didn't know him. She couldn't. She was barely a month old when he left, and only recently had she started playing shy. She didn't want anything to do with him, wouldn't let him be the one to carry her places, to feed her, to change her.

So, I'm the one who ends up taking her, doing all the same things I did before just so I don't have to hear her crying. Which just makes Mark more annoyed, as he keeps insisting the only way she will accept him is if he does the things

It's not that I'm trying to block him out. I just don't feel like listening to her scream all day.

It took about a week before he pointed out the ways he thought I could improve my daily life.

Why don't you keep the wipes over on this table?

You should do the laundry every night, that way you won't get overwhelmed.

Why do you get groceries so often? You should make a list and have a meal plan and then you'd only have to go once a week.

How do you explain that your way is just comfortable now? That laundry isn't my priority and sometimes I just need to get out of the damn house and see other adults, and getting groceries is a good excuse to do that?

I try to remind myself it's a hard transition for him, to be in command of people and then come home and not feel like he is in command of me. My head knows this, but my heart is just angry. He's the one that left, left me to look after his infant daughter on my own, and then he thinks he can come back and tell me the ways I didn't do it right?

I. Don't. Fucking. Think. So.

So instead, we've been butting heads. Sometimes, he'll back off but most of the time, it ends in frustrated huffing and storming off.

Tonight, the blowout comes when I put Tori in a car seat and grabbing my keys. I had noticed a few things we were out of and she'd been fussing a bit, so I figured a late evening run to the store might do us both some good. Gets me out of the house when some weeks I feel like a blob, and give her a change of scenery so hopefully she's sleeping by the time I'm back.

Mark pokes his head out from behind the TV that's always on now.

"What are you doing?" His voice is combative, right off the bat and it grates on my nerves.

"I'm headed out to Wal-Mart. We're missing a few things I want for dinner tomorrow, so we're going to go grab them."

Mark stares at me for a moment in confusion as I put my shoes on.

"That doesn't make any sense, Meg! You see that, right? Why don't you wait and go tomorrow if you have to? You probably don't even need it then; there's more than enough damn food in this house already!"

I don't really have an answer for him. The thing is, it doesn't make much sense for me to go out that night for any reason other than to get out. I don't have a good response except to say I am going because I want to. Then I do.

When I get home, he isn't there. A cab drops him off late in the night, I had fallen asleep on the couch feeding Victoria. I don't say a word as I watch him stumble in the door and towards the bedroom in the dark without noticing me. I am sure he'd come back out looking for me when he realizes I am not where he thought I'd be, but soon there is silence in the house again.

He had fallen asleep without even noticing I wasn't in our bed.

11

MARK

PRESENT

The nurses finally kick me out of Megan's room sometime around midnight. I'd been staring at her in the same position for hours after she fell back asleep. Not moving, hardly breathing, just staring.

I don't need you.

I feel almost drunk with exhaustion as I walk out to the parking lot. I throw my bag in the backseat of the car I rented when I got to the airport. I could have called someone for a ride, but I didn't even think. It's yellow, some compact thing with satellite radio and leather seats. At least, that's what the sales guy told me while I was busy signing the papers. It was an hour drive up to this hospital and I never even turned the radio on.

I drive on autopilot to our house. Tucked in the back of an off-base neighbourhood we picked less than two years ago, the quaint two story has the tiny front porch Megan wanted and the decent-sized garage I wouldn't do without. I stare at the house for a long while. With the five days or so we had to pick a place, we did a pretty amazing job of it. Megan had loved the open kitchen and the tiny ensuite.

I want to say I love the house too, but I'd be guessing. The place doesn't even look like home to me. I've only spent maybe five of the eighteen months we've owned it living there.

I'm parked in the driveway when I realize I don't have a key to get in. I didn't bring my car to the airport in Toronto and so my keys are sitting on the counter in the little long-term-stay hotel suite I've been living in.

I can't get into my own home.

If I can even call it that.

When did this happen? I want to say it was when I left for Toronto without them, but I have a feeling it started before then. Was it that last deployment? The last move? When did I become a stranger in my own home? To my own family?

I guess I could call Cheryl, see if she has a key at her place I could come get, but it's almost one in the morning and she's got six kids there. I'm not ready to face her, or them, either. All that can wait until morning.

I flip open my phone. I hadn't even turned it on from the airplane yet, so when it powers up, I have several messages. I know a bunch of the guys have heard I was coming home; the Army is smaller than we think and word travels fast. I don't want to talk to anyone, though. I recognize one of the numbers and I call it back without even listening to the voicemail.

"Mark."

Bill answers the phone on the first ring. It probably sits right by his bed. He's still the sergeant major of the company so his Blackberry is always right there, even at one a.m. on a Wednesday. I'm grateful. Bill lives alone and is, thankfully, not one for small talk. Or any talk. Which is perfect.

"Hey, Bill."

"You in town?"

"I am. And, uh…"

"Come on by. I'll throw some sheets on the futon."

"Thanks, man."

The line clicks, and I throw the phone back on the seat next to me.

It's a short drive to the townhouse Bill lives in. It's just a small place, close to base with a bedroom for him and one for his son when he comes up to visit from Nova Scotia. Bill and the kid's mother split years ago and she took him back to where she called home. Bill was too defeated to argue, and anyways, he knew with his schedule, he'd never be able to offer primary guardianship of the boy. Instead, now he sees him once or twice a year at visits that are getting more and more awkward as the kid grows up. I know Bill is steeling himself for the day his son is old enough to choose not to want to come at all anymore.

A chill runs through me. I never thought I could imagine what that kind of separation from your family could feel like, but I never thought I'd be sleeping on a friend's couch in the same city as my wife, either.

Bill has the door open before I even get up the front step. Seeing him there, shirtless with his plaid pyjama pants hanging low on his hips, reading glasses on his nose and a bottle of Keith's in one hand. I even manage a little smile. If the younger members of the company could see him now, leaning on the door frame with one hand in his pocket, they wouldn't believe it. At just a bit taller than I am, with tattoos forming a solid wall of colour up both arms before stopping sharply at his shoulders, and a fitness level even the young privates are envious of, Bill is known to be a stickler for discipline in the ranks and can scare the shit out of almost anyone just with a look. Myself included.

In his off time, though, he's pensive and might even be considered soft spoken. An avid reader, his office is lined with military biographies and historical dramas. He's a hard ass, sure, but for all the right reasons. He cares for the men who serve under him and he wants them to succeed. His patented, "I'm not mad, I'm disappointed" speech is legendary at the battalion. It was a privilege to lead beside him in Afghanistan, especially when it all went sideways.

Bill doesn't say a word as I walk up, just steps out of the doorway, so I can come in and closes the door behind me. As I throw my bag onto the futon in the small living room that has a pile of sheets, a pillow, and a ranger blanket piled on the end, he comes back from the kitchen with another Keith's and hands it to me. I notice he's already opened it, so I can't refuse.

"See her yet?" he asks, plopping unceremoniously onto the recliner in the corner. I flop onto the futon and bring the bottle to my lips. The beer is cold, and the first gulp reminds me I haven't eaten since breakfast.

"Ya." I just stare for a minute and Bill says nothing.

"She's out of it, she was only awake for a couple minutes. She… didn't really want me there."

"I doubt that. You surprised her. She didn't call you for a reason."

"That's the problem! I should have known about this." I take a long drink from my bottle and put the beer down; it sits too heavy in my stomach.

"Tell me something. Would you have expected her to call you overseas if she had the flu?" Bill looks at me a little too intently, and it makes me pick up my beer again just so I have something in my hands.

"No, of course not, she can deal with that. But I'm not overseas. I'm in another province."

"Okay, then what if she had pneumonia? A broken bone?"

"She wouldn't need me for those things." I'm starting to sound defensive, even to myself.

"Ya, so where's the line, Mark? When was she supposed to let you know? If keeping some things to herself is best only up until a point, where is that point? How bad is bad enough? How close is close enough?"

"I don't… She has CANCER, Bill!"

Bill doesn't recoil from my outburst. In fact, he doesn't even blink. He just slowly puts his bottle down and stands up, headed to the door.

"A strong woman can hide even the loudest truth if she's spent enough time thinking it's what her family needs." He gives me one last look before he shuts off the light in the kitchen and heads upstairs.

Dammit.

12

MEGAN

WINTER 2002

*G*oodness this place stinks.

I don't even think it's just all the people crammed in here, either. It smells faintly of musty uniforms and the diesel of the vehicles outside, dirty diapers, and sweat. But I think what makes it the worst is that underlying smell of terror, anger, heartbreak.

Goodbye.

This place smells like goodbyes.

Families all wait around, while tables set up with the final paperwork are scattered throughout the building. A giant room, with hard bleacher seats that kids run up and down, oblivious really to what's happening, there's the odd squeal of laughter and intermittently a baby cries.

There's not a lot of conversation, though. Whispers between couples as they sit huddled together and wait for the final call. The muted voices of the various soldiers making the final plans. In one corner, single guys in uniform stand around looking a little more excited than apprehensive. They don't have any goodbyes to give before they leave here. There's nothing to make this moment any less thrilling for them.

I imagine heading to war is easier when you don't have to kiss anyone goodbye, but I don't really know. I've never been where they are.

I'm always the one left behind.

The one keeping the house, the kids.

The one there when he gets home from saving the world.

Mark and I are coming up on our third anniversary this spring, but it most definitely won't be spent together. Which is about par for the course so far. He missed the first six months of Tori's life while he was in Kosovo and now she' on my hip, a loud, rambunctious almost two-year-old who, in three months, will welcome her little brother into the world. Without her daddy.

Even after he got back from that first deployment, he always seems to be off somewhere. Our time together is precious. Last year, we took a one-year-old to Disney World as though she has any hope of remembering the thousands we spent. Guilt is such a powerful motivator, and some days I feel like Victoria's life so far has been a series of extended periods of an absent father and a flustered mother, punctuated by short, excitement-filled moments where we try to cram life into the times we're together.

I absently pat my rounded belly and Tori does the same. That second baby sure doesn't take its time before it starts showing. I swear I was in maternity pants the day that second line showed up on the pregnancy test. At least we had planned for it this time. After taking a little over a year to adjust to having Tori around, we decided to just take the plunge. We had no way of knowing this was coming, no way of anticipating a war on the horizon until I sat horrified and watched the plane hit that second tower. Mark wasn't home for that either, away somewhere training. Instead, a knock on the door and our neighbour Michelle, a bubbly woman with bouncy red hair and never-ending smile, walked right in to the TV room and sat with me without saying a word. We held hands by the time we watch the people jumping. Both of us in tears for the unimaginable loss, both of us married to soldiers and knowing our lives would never be the same. It had been the first time I experienced how sometimes the military creates family where you didn't know you had it.

So now I'm going to do this birth on my own. The best laid plans, as they say. If there's one thing the military has taught me since that very first month, it's that it's best I don't try to plan anything. Chances are no matter what I try, I'll still end up pregnant with a toddler on my hip, watching my husband leave for an indeterminate amount of time to the desert.

Or something like that.

I already feel about as big as I did when I was eight months along with Tori. My feet, my ankles, my face is swollen. I turn and glance at a few of the other ladies here that are clearly also expecting, their adorable little bumps the only indication. They glow.

I, however, just look like an angry beachball with arms and legs.

We've known this day was coming since the world watched the enemy declare war in New York almost five months ago. Five months is a very long time to wait for the 'any day now' deployment. A long time to think about what war looks like, think about what alone looks like, to realize that this time he won't just be missing half a year of his child's life like before; he'll be missing that moment his child enters the world, too.

I'm not the first woman to give birth while her husband is at war.

Knowing that doesn't in fact make it easier.

Mark stands up at one of the tables, running his hand

through what I've now realized is his always slightly too long hair over and over while he talks to some of the younger guys. Despite the tick I know him well enough to know is mostly nerves, he looks strong and confident. He must, he's one of their leaders. One of the ones who will be responsible for them, for their safety, to their families. When I see him, he looks like the almost twenty-seven-year-old kid I know he is, the same guy who dances to Sir Mix-a-Lot with his baby daughter and refuses to eat oatmeal because mush for breakfast just isn't right, apparently.

I don't see a soldier, or a leader. I don't see whatever an infantry captain is supposed to be. I can't even picture him firing his weapon. I can't imagine him leading his men to war.

There's so much uncertainty here. We don't know exactly what they'll be doing. We don't know when they'll be coming back. We don't know much of anything. How do you even begin to know what the first combat deployment in decades looks like? War is something you think you can picture in your head, but it's not something you can ever understand. Especially when you husband is standing there, ready to head out the door.

Mark saunters back over to us and my heart seizes at the look on his face.

It's time.

It's been five months of waiting and hours here in this room.

I thought I was ready.

I'm not ready.

We've spent the past while just planning, preparing, trying to be as proactive as we can be. My sister was a godsend when he was in Kosovo, helping with Tori and keeping me company. I don't know what I'd do without her, and imagining the months I have ahead, the baby that's coming with or without his dad, and the toddler that isn't going to care that Mom got no sleep the night before, I am so grateful to not being doing this completely alone. While motherhood has seemed isolating at times and I've lost touch with more than a few friends, I've gained a best friend in her. Erika is still around, she tends to go through men like outfits but never stops checking in, and helping when I need her. There's my neighbour Michelle. A handful of others I know will do what they can.

It's not the same, though, without Mark. This is his life. His family. His son. And he won't be here for one of those moments.

Mark walks over to the bench and shoulders his bag before standing in front of me. I'm not crying. After five months of hurry up and wait, the tears are all gone. I'm just resigned. So, when he looks at me and I see the pain etched on his face, I don't expect the burning to start in my eyes again.

He picks Tori up out of my arms first and hugs her tight. She's smiling when he pulls back and looks in her face.

"I have to go away awhile, like we said. You are going to be really good for Mommy and the new baby when he comes, right?" Tori's face is just simple innocence. She has no idea what's going on. She just smiles and gives a vigorous nod, her dark, loose curls that mirror her father's bouncing into her face with each shake of her head.

He kisses her cheek and gently places her on the first riser where she promptly plops on her bum and reaches for her snacks. I wish I was as calm as her. I wish I could be as oblivious.

Before he straightens, Mark rests his forehead against my belly. Both his hands rub over the top of my bump and I can hear his soft whispers. I feel almost like I'm somehow intruding on his moment with his son, and I am almost grateful I can't hear whatever words he's saying to him.

Eventually, he stands and cups my face in his hands. I can't help but lean into him, resting my chin on his palms. He brushes away the hair that's fallen onto my cheek and kisses the skin he exposed. Resting his forehead against mine, he looks down at me with worried eyes that are glassy but dry. This isn't our first rodeo and there's absolutely no chance he'll shed a tear here, with his men watching on.

"We've got this, right?"

I can't help but bite back a laugh at the idea we're going into this together. What we have are two very different realities. I'm going to be home, with a messy house, a terror of a toddler, and a new baby.

He's going to be dusty, hot, and very possibly shot at.

Oh, God.

I can't think about that part.

"Ya, babe. We've got this." I give him my best smile, though I know it's nowhere near my eyes. Neither is his.

"I don't know how long it will be before I can call you. I'll try to, though, as soon as I can. Don't watch the news, okay? I know you will want to, but just don't. All you need to worry about is you and Tor and our son. That's all. Everything else can wait, okay? Don't worry about me. Don't worry about work. You just worry about you and our babies.

"I love you, doll. I love you more than anything else in this world. I'll be home before you know it."

I blink a few times to keep the tears at bay and he kisses me, just softly. A lingering touch on my lips that I feel long after the moment he steps back. He turns then, his pack on his shoulder, and he walks out the door to the bus.

He doesn't look back.

Not once.

I know because I don't stop watching until the bus pulls away.

* * *

Cheryl is a much more useful birth coach than Mark was.

It's a few weeks early but Baby Lawson doesn't want to wait. Turns out all that swelling was my blood pressure and at thirty-

FIGHT FOR HOME

six weeks, the doctor decides it's time to get this little leech out of me. Some gel and an IV later and we don't seem to be getting anywhere.

"Do you want to move around before the epidural goes in?" Cheryl asks. She's already done this three times now. Three times. Colby is only a few months old now, and she swears she is done but honestly, I think Paul just likes her knocked up, and whether she admits it or not, she loves every moment of motherhood.

I, on the other hand, am just tired.

I get up and wander the halls for a moment. We joke about each room, about the loud fathers yelling the countdown for each contraction. About the nervous grandparents in the waiting room. About the smack of my flip flops on the hospital floor as my swollen feet take each step. When we make it back to the room, she helps me back up on the bed and she picks her book up. She tried to get the TV turned on, but it doesn't seem to be working.

Cheryl is passing me some ice chips when the anesthesiologist finally comes in.

"We're going to get you an epidural, yes?" she says with far too much enthusiasm. I wish these people would realize that being super happy around me doesn't make me super happy. It just makes me annoyed

Literally everything makes me annoyed.

"That would be awesome, thank you."

As she prepares all her implements, none of which look particularly inviting, she makes some small talk, asking about baby names, siblings, birth partners. When I tell her my sister is filling in for my husband who is in Afghanistan, a shadow crosses her face for just a moment before she continues smiling. I wonder briefly what that was about, but I chalk it up to bad feelings about the military, or annoyance that I'm having to do it without him. Not everyone I've encountered has had positive thoughts about the military. Right now, I could care less about her political ideology, I just want the damn drugs.

As I'm getting settled back into the bed with the drug line in my back, I ask the nurse about the phone line in my room. It was supposed to be hooked up right away, so Mark could call. I sent word to the Rear Party back at base, the ones in charge of helping those of us back home, to let him know the baby was coming. I'd hoped he'd call sooner than later but I've heard nothing.

"He'll call, Megan. He will. I'm sure wherever he is, he's doing his best. Right now, you just need to focus on you and that baby that needs to come out." Cheryl rubs her thumb across the top of the hand she's holding. Tori is at her and Paul's place, along with her three, Layne, Danica, and Colby. Last I heard, Paul was attempting to make four different dinners before putting them to bed. The thought of my lanky and bookish brother-in-law trying to corral all those kids into a bedtime is hilarious; there's a good chance he'll get about as much sleep as I will tonight.

As the hours pass, it gets harder and harder, but I make no progress. I don't miss the nervous looks from the nurses and they keep coming in and checking the monitors they've connected to all parts of me and even one all the way inside attached to the baby's head. By early morning, I almost wish I could use that line to pull the friggin boy out. I'm exhausted, everything hurts, and nothing seems to be working.

Eventually, the doctor comes in and I can see by the look on his face I'm out of options.

"Megan, we've tried different positions and we've left you on the IV as long as we can, but I'm afraid your blood pressure has reached levels we aren't comfortable with, and the little one is showing some signs of distress. I recommend we take you in now for a C-section. You already have an epidural in, so we won't have to put you under, but we do need to get you into the OR sooner than later."

I look over to Cheryl and she squeezes my hand. I still haven't heard from Mark.

"What if Mark calls while I'm in there?" My voice is considerably higher than it needs to be. I know I sound hysterical over the wrong things. I guess I should be more worried about the major surgery he's suggesting, but they must understand that missing his call would devastate me. The doctor and Cheryl exchange a glance I can't determine, but I'm not in any shape to try to figure out their expressions.

"I'll be right here. I'll answer if he calls and I won't let him hang up until he talks to you. I promise."

"Tell him I'm sorry…"

"Megan, this isn't your fault. You did amazing. Sometimes, it just happens this way. He'll be so proud of you no matter what. Go. I'll be right here. I love you, sis."

Cheryl doesn't let go of my hand until the bed pulls me away. The OR is oddly quiet, and the beeping of the monitors seems that much louder in the cavernous white room. They adjust my drugs, restrain my hands and legs, and poke me a few times to be sure I can't feel anything before they get to work. It feels like pressure, tugging and pulling for several long moments before I hear a cry.

They bring him over to me so I can see him; his dark hair is already long enough to be matted to his head, with big blue eyes wide open and staring at me.

"Congratulations, Mama. Does he have a name?"

I stare another moment before I find the words. This whole moment feels wrong. There's a huge presence missing in the room. Finally, I realize the nurse is still waiting on my answer.

"Yes." My voice is rough. "His name is Vincent Anthony Lawson." We had decided months ago, and gave our son Mark's father's name as his middle name.

There's a blur of activity but when I make it back into the room while they're cleaning him up and checking him over, I hear Cheryl's voice.

"Oh! She's back. Just hold on, okay? Just one more minute, I can hear them bringing her back!"

She's holding out the phone to me as soon as I stop moving and she holds it up to my ear.

"Mark?" I can hear the static of the satellite line before I hear his voice.

"Megan? Hey, doll, I'm so sorry I couldn't call right away. Cheryl told me you had to have a C-section. I really do wish I was there. Are you okay?"

I wait a moment for the delay to catch up before I answer.

"It's okay, I'm good. Cheryl was great. Vincent is perfect. We did fine here, you don't need to worry."

There's a long silence. Longer than the delay.

"Oh."

I wait, thinking there will be more but there isn't.

Oh?

I brush it off and keep going, giving him all the particulars of his newborn son, his height and weight and the way his hair is already almost in his gorgeous blue eyes.

"I wish you could see him, Mark. I'll have Cheryl print some photos and put them in the mail right away."

"Have you seen the news, Meg?"

That's a weird question. I just had an effin baby. I haven't exactly been glued to CTV.

"No, I haven't exactly had time for TV this last bit, Mark." As soon as the words are out of my mouth, I see Cheryl flinch. I wonder if the TV really wasn't working when all the nurses glance over nervously.

"Why? What's going on?" I say it as the same time I hear Mark's voice follow the delay.

"I'm okay. Just, when you do see the news, remember I'm okay. All right?"

Now I know the TV has been kept off for a reason, and I remember every strange look I've seen on the people around me since late last night.

"You're scaring me, Mark."

"I'm okay, Megan. I do have to go and I'm so sorry, but I've already been on the phone longer than I should. I'll call, and we can talk for longer really soon. I'm so proud of you. I can't wait to meet Vince. You've got this. I love you."

I start to tell him I love him too, but I hear the line cut out before I get the words out of my mouth. When I hang up the phone, I look pointedly at Cheryl.

"I didn't want to worry you with everything else, Meg. There was an incident in Afghanistan yesterday. The news says four soldiers were killed."

My breath hitches as my heart reaches my mouth and Cheryl grabs my hand as the nurse places Vince in my arms.

"He's okay, Megan. He's okay, and Vince is okay. You've got this."

Casualties.

There's been casualties.

Because this is really war.

I stare down at Vince's tiny fingers as they open and close around the blanket.

I wish I was as sure as everyone else that I've got this.

13

MARK

SUMMER 2002

Landing at this island paradise, one would think I'd be excited, but I'm mostly just exhausted.
We've made it.

This might not have been my first deployment, but it was our first deployment to war. There's a different atmosphere here than there was in Kosovo. Probably because while there aren't any actual empty seats, there might as well be, and the ones who aren't making this trip today have a louder voice on this plane than the ones of us still here.

Checking into the hotel here, I look at the rowdys around me, already looking for the bar, and I chuckle at the government's idea of decompression. I guess a few days here before we head home is supposed to get six months of war without a break out of our system.

I doubt that's going to be effective, but no one asked me, so I guess we'll see. Either way, I won't turn up my nose at three days in a tropical paradise.

We have a few seminars to take, and it looks like there's some tours and other activities that are supposed to fill our time, but I can't bring myself to care tonight. I'm with the rest, I just want to find my room and then find a bar. Full stop.

Once I'm all checked in, with Dennis here as my roommate, I'm finishing up in the bathroom after taking a moment just to enjoy sitting on an actual toilet, when the door opens and Dennis stands there, grinning like a Cheshire cat.

That can't be good.

"Jeez, Mark, cover that shit up!" He uses whatever's in his hands to cover his eyes in mock horror. I hadn't bothered throwing clothes back on yet since I was about to get changed to go out anyways. I only have like three pieces of civilian clothes as it is, so we're going to have to go shopping and it's been awhile since I could let it all hang loose for more than a few hurried seconds. The air conditioning feels like heaven. I'm not covering up for some idiot who wants to pretend we haven't seen each other's junk a thousand times before.

"You're the asshole walking in on me in the bathroom. You're lucky I'm off the shitter."

"Ya, I've seen enough of that to last me a few lifetimes. Anyways, I brought you a little something the guys picked up for you to wear. They just dropped it off, you'll love it." There's a twinkle in his eyes that I'm not too fond of when he throws the t-shirt at me.

It's a hideous peach colour, with tiny palm trees that look a lot like little dicks all over it. Right front and center in big letters are the words, "Hey, Sailor!" in baby blue.

I'm stunned speechless for a minute until the sound of Dennis laughing so hard he sounds like he's choking snaps me out of it.

"I guess they picked it up at the gift shop downstairs and thought of you. I'm sworn to secrecy on who dropped it off, though."

I stare at the abomination a few more seconds before I decide.

"Fuck it." I flip it in my hands and start to pull it on. Now Dennis has slid all the way onto the bathroom floor, tears down his face.

"You're actually going to wear that?"

"My mom taught me it was rude to refuse a gift. Of course, I am. You're the idiots that will have to be seen with me all night."

Dennis is still laughing to himself, louder every time he looks over at me, as we make our way outside. I give him one last shove in the lobby and he ends up ass over teakettle into a planter, scrambling back up and chasing me through the giant front doors to the outside.

The heat isn't as intense as it was in Kandahar, but the humidity almost takes the air from my lungs. It's been so long that we've been breathing in nothing but dry air and questionable dust, I had almost forgotten what it felt like to have moisture on my skin. Just being out in a sun that doesn't feel like it wants to kill me, without all my gear on, is already relaxing.

And weirdly the opposite of that, too.

I realize halfway to the restaurant that I forgot to call Megan. I had promised I would when I got here so we could have a real conversation, something we haven't had the chance to do over the past six months, but between just enjoying the cool air and Dennis bringing the damn shirt, it totally slipped my mind and it's too late now. The complete ruckus that takes over the restaurant when I walk in wearing this terrible shirt is legendary and it is only the start of a night that quickly loses track of any attempt at civility.

We soon move from the restaurant to bar after bar. Somewhere along the way there was a jet ski excursion. At least I think there was. There's over five hundred Canadian soldiers taking over this island tonight and it's only getting rougher.

Maybe there *was* some wisdom in letting us blow off some steam here before we subject ourselves to the real world.

Everywhere we go, I pull a lot of stares. I'm long past too drunk to care and the boys are having a great time showing me off to anyone that will pay their loud, drunk selves any attention, jokingly trying to get me a 'date' with any sailor on the island.

So ya, it's gotten a little messy.

I've lost count of the number of drinks I've had by the time Dennis and about a half-dozen other guys find ourselves wandering the streets in the general direction of the hotel. I have no idea what time it is. A voice in my head keeps reminding me I need to call Megan still, but I keep pushing it back down. Besides, that voice was conspicuously quiet in the strip club we just left. I mean, I kept my hands to myself of course. I'd never consider a mistake like that no matter what shape I'm in, but man, it's been a long six months. I miss my wife.

It helps that whenever I close my eyes, I see the only photo I've gotten this deployment, of Megan holding newborn Vince with Tori sitting next to them in the hospital. She's red faced and sweaty, her hair a white-blonde helmet stuck to her head and all over her face, her eyes exhausted.

She looks gorgeous and my heart seizes every time I think about how I'm not in the photo at all.

By the time I meet him, Vince will be almost two months old. I don't even know how to 'meet' a newborn, especially *my* newborn. He won't know me. And as he grows up, he won't remember that I missed him coming into the world. He'll have no memory of these first weeks where he didn't know me.

I will remember though, and so will Megan.

I can still remember her voice on the phone. "We did fine."

She had my son without me, and it turns out she didn't need me. That hurts more than I'd like.

God, I miss them.

I stop walking, well, stumbling, when I realize Dennis isn't with me anymore. I look back to see him curling up on a bench off the sidewalk.

"Hell no, big boy. C'mon. Hotel isn't too much farther."

"Just leave me." He gives a sad wave in my direction. "Ima gonna jus seep heee."

I stare at him a minute. His brown hair is curly, and he let it grow since we've been gone. There were no barbers around and he insisted they couldn't make him just shave it off himself. Instead, he has this crazy ridiculous mop that falls into his eyes, just like he had in Kosovo. He's built like a brick shit house, even with the weight we lost this tour. He's got the same ugly as sin cargo shorts on that I do, ones we bought in Dubai on R&R months ago. And a button-up Hawaiian shirt, blue with yellow flowers that makes his Greek olive skin look even darker. Hell, with his complexion after the six months we just spent in the desert and him with that constant sunburn, his skin is almost maroon. That leather look to him has started to just represent what he looks like on deployment.

"I leave you here, I'm trading shirts with you. How bad do you want to spend the night outside, passed out alone, in a shirt covered in palm tree dicks?"

That gets his attention and he laughs as he pulls himself to almost standing. The rest of the guys we were walking with are long gone so we make quite the pair, neither of us particularly upright as we stumble our way back to our room.

By the time we fall in the door, I can see the faintest light in the sky through the open window.

Shit. Morning isn't going to be pretty for whatever workshops the Army has planned for us.

I fall into bed, flopping around over the sheets as I attempt to take my shorts off. I hear Dennis doing the same on his bed before he stills. I'm halfway to sleep when I hear him from across the room.

"How do we go home from this?" His voice is harsh, showing the effects of a night of drinking and yelling.

"I don't know, man, I just want to see my wife and my kids. Have sex. Maybe buy a boat. Take the kids fishing. Sail on the boat with my wife. Have sex on the boat…" I'm rambling, my brain already mostly shut off for the night. He grunts, and I'm so far gone I don't even know for sure I hear him respond.

"How am I supposed to do it alone?"

14

MEGAN

PRESENT

When I wake again, everything hurts just a little less. Except my heart.

Mark is gone, and it takes some convincing on my part to believe he was here at all. I wonder where he went, how long he'll be in town, if he'll help with the kids. I wonder why he came and who told him to come. I wonder if he came for me, or because someone told him he had to.

Staff are just dropping off a soggy-looking breakfast to my room when Cheryl walks in with two Tim Horton's cups.

"Hey, sleepyhead. You know you scared the shit out of us. I called this morning and the nurses said you were finally awake, so I brought you a tea." She plops down with a thud next to me. She's got her long blonde hair, just a few shades darker than mine, pulled into a messy bun, with faded jeans. Her oversized sweater is still stretched thin over her chest, barely containing the overabundance that is the combination of our genetics and her almost constant state of breastfeeding. She and Paul insist that after having Dylan almost two years ago, they're done with four, but I'll believe it when I see it. Cheryl seems to thrive with little ones underfoot.

"Hey," I croak. My voice sounds foreign, even to me. "Where are Tori and Vince?"

"Home with Paul. It's Saturday, he's going to take them to Kid Quarters to blow off some steam."

I supposed if anyone could handle six kids at the play gym, it would be Paul. With his buttoned-down look, boyish smile, and bookish glasses, even as tall as he is one would think he was a pushover, but that man can lay down the law with kids like no one I've ever seen. He reminds me of the Pied Piper.

"Mark was here."

Cheryl looks up a moment before she nods.

"I know. He came by the house this morning and took the kids out for breakfast. I gave him a key to your place, he forgot his I guess. He said he'll be back here this morning. He just needed to change and shower, and deal with his rental car."

I hadn't even considered how he'd gotten here last night, or where he'd gone after. I wonder where he spent the night. I briefly consider whose bed he might have been in even though my heart doesn't really believe I have reason to. I hate the uncertainty that has corroded our relationship. I don't even know when it all creeped its way in.

"He said he ended up at a friend's house last night, someone named Bill. He didn't want to wake us for a key," Cheryl says softly, like she can read my mind. I search my memories for someone named Bill. He must mean Bill Hurst, his old sergeant major. That guy always scared me a little, though his mustache fascinated me. I wondered what it would look like if he didn't wax it to points on the end. Would the tips just fall, or would the sides end in little puffballs of hair?

That's probably not important right now.

"I didn't call him, just so you know. I wanted to, but you said not to, and I didn't. I'm not sorry he's here, though. He should be. He should have been here all along."

I don't know who did call him, but as soon as she says that, the guilt is back. I can't believe he had to come home. I can only imagine how disappointed he must be to have to deal with me instead of focus on school like he's supposed to. I've been doing this for nine years and I've never, ever asked him to come back home for me. I feel like a failure, and I need to convince him he can head back. I've got this.

What right does he have, anyways, to decide for me when I need him? I've done just fine without him. If he thinks he's just going to come strolling back and act like the white knight, he's got another thing coming.

"I can't believe he just decided to come home without asking me if I needed him to."

"Of course, I came home!"

Mark stands in the doorway, wearing crumpled jeans and a faded grey Henley; the dark circles under his eyes only accentuate the piercing look in them. Cheryl stands wordlessly and heads towards the door, her shoulder colliding with Mark as she walks out. She makes no attempt to step around him. They've rarely seen eye to eye. His quick departures and long absences a sticking point in their relationship. No matter how many times I'd explain to her that it was just his job, she could never see it as less than abandonment.

Mark stays by the door for a long moment, just watching me. He looks defeated and he picks absently at the cup in his hand, running his short fingernail across the seam over and over. Finally, he puts it down on the small table next to my discarded, barely eaten breakfast and sits down where Cheryl had been, thoughtlessly bouncing his left leg on the ball of his foot. I never could pinpoint exactly when his need for constant movement took him over, but it's been years since I've seen him sit still.

Shouldn't that have been something I noticed, when he started to change? Was it the war? The stress at home? Was it just part of the man he grew into, this high-stress ball of energy who's constantly on the move, even when he's sitting still?

"I picked up Tori and Vince today. We had breakfast, but Paul decided he would take them all to some indoor gym so I could spend time with you."

"Cheryl told me. They must have been excited to see you."

"Ya, they were. Tori is acting like a little mother, always fussing over Vince. She needs to leave the poor guy alone instead of bossing him around."

"Tori is just fine. She's an eight-year-old girl, that's how they are. She's not hurting him," I snap back. He hasn't even been home a full day and already he's on this? He can go to hell if he thinks I'll just let him swoop back in, insult my parenting, and discipline my kids like he knows anything about them.

"Vince is five, he doesn't need two mothers."

"Maybe he does, since he doesn't really have a *father* around, does he?"

Mark goes quiet and once again, we just sit in the room, looking at each other like strangers. When did this happen, that I ended up married to someone I don't even know?

"Look… that's not what I came here to talk about. Meg, you need to tell me more about what happened. I mean, I read your chart, but it doesn't make a lot of sense to me. What happened? When did this start?" I can hear the other question hanging in the air between us, but he doesn't ask it.

Why didn't you tell me?

I start to explain it all to him but when I open my mouth, it's that silent question I answer instead.

"Look, it's not as big a deal as it seems right now, Mark. I didn't want you to have to come home for nothing, and I still don't understand why you're here now. Cheryl has the kids. I won't be here too much longer before I can head home and take them back. I might have to take a break from work for a bit, but I don't need you home for this. There's nothing you can do anyways."

Mark stands up, his entire body rigid. He looks down at me and his face is twisted, "My WIFE has CANCER, Megan. Of course, I'm going to be here. How does it look that you've been going through all this alone?" He runs his hands through his hair, the same frustrated move he's made in all the years I've known him.

"Of course. You're worried about how it looks. Well, I'm sorry I assumed you'd want to be focused on work. Sorry I did all this on my own when you're the one who leaves, not me. Sorry I made you *look bad* by having cancer."

"Dammit, Meg, you know that's not what I meant!" Mark's hand goes through his hair again and now he's pacing across the room.

The door behind him opens and I see the stiffness in him at the unexpected sound. It lasts only a half second, but my eyes have learned to read those cues from him. I look over at the source of the noise as my nurse clicks the door behind her. She has a sour look on her face and directs it right towards Mark.

"Excuse me. My patient is exhausted and has a severe infection. Maybe it's time she got a bit more rest? You can come back later."

Mark glares her down for a moment. "Visitors are allowed until eleven tonight, I'm staying here with my wife. If she wants some rest, she can go to sleep."

"I don't see how she could with someone as inconsiderate as *you* in here," the nurse mumbles under her breath before writing a few things on her chart and ducking back out. I'm grateful Mark keeps his mouth shut until the tap of her shoes moves down the hall.

"Meg, do you want me to go?"

I don't. Not really. I look at him and for the first time in so long, I crave him. I crave his arms around me from behind. I crave the feel of his breath on the back of my neck. Needing him is a luxury I stopped allowing myself years ago and suddenly, for a moment, I remember how good it felt. Right up until it didn't.

I shake those thoughts from my head and I really see him, and he looks so tired. The deep black circles under his eyes almost pull his whole face down. He needs to get some rest. He needs to go back to Toronto and finish his work. He doesn't need to be here. If he won't go back to school, at the very least he may as well get some sleep.

"Just go home and get some sleep, Mark. I'm fine."

He just stares. He stares for far too long, his eyes searching my face as though he has lost something important somewhere in the lines. Eventually, he grabs his jacket and keys and walks closer, gently kissing my forehead and heading to the door.

"Okay, Megan. If that's what you want."

I want to yell after him that what I want has never factored into the equation, and it's completely different from what I need. What *he* needs. But instead, I just watch the door click behind him and wonder with all I am when it started being easier to sleep when he's gone.

15

MARK

SPRING 2003

I can't find my rifle.
It should be right here.
IT SHOULD BE RIGHT HERE.

My hands flail around me, reaching out, trying to grab hold of the hard surface of the rifle that should be right next to me but it's not. I can't figure out why until I grab onto something soft next to me.

Some*one* soft next to me.

"We're at home, Mark. Your rifle isn't here. Go back to sleep," she mumbles at me before turning away and taking most of the blanket with her. I can see over her shoulder now the two raven-haired toddlers sleeping next to her. This isn't the first time I've woken her in a mad search for my C7. I doubt by the time she really wakes up she'll even remember it happened. I can't decide if that's a good thing or just a sign of how bad I've messed with her over the years.

We're on the floor of the living room, along with a couple

fleece blankets and a giant air mattress. The packers come tomorrow, and Megan didn't want them packing dirty sheets, so she washed everything yesterday and made us all sleep together here on the floor on our last night in this house. The kids thought it was exciting, like a fun camp out.

I've done enough camping. I don't know that I'll ever get the appeal of sleeping on the ground for fun. I glance at my watch, it's only a little after five a.m., but there's no sense in lying here any longer. I can't fall back to sleep. I roll myself as gently as I can off the air mattress, the loss of my weight bouncing the other three who are still sleeping. They barely notice. I make myself some coffee and head outside, sitting on the cool concrete of the front step. The chill reminds me I'm in nothing but my plaid pyjama pants, but I can't be bothered to care all that much.

This is the house Megan and I came home to that first night. It's nothing special, just a little three-bedroom bungalow I bought with the money my parents left me. The tap on the kitchen sink has leaked for over a year and there's stains on the bedroom carpet. Our little single-car garage barely manages to fit the minivan, and the postage stamp of a yard has just the one sad little tree that looks half dead, even in the middle of the summer. It seemed great when I bought it, it was just me and Dennis who moved in as a roommate for a bit. Now it just looks cramped and small with a family of four. I don't have much attachment to it and I'm glad for the upgrade the move will give us.

Today, the movers will pack our things. Tomorrow, they load the truck. Friday, we clean this place up and sign the papers. Saturday morning, we drive out of this province and all the way to St. Jean, Quebec, to our new house and my new job.

I've been at Battalion, ever since I was a brand new 2nd lieutenant just getting my bearings. The idea of leaving, while it's just part of the job, scares me more than any deployment I've been on. I'm supposed to just switch, from leading men to teaching them, from training myself to training others. My French will certainly be tested, not to mention my administration skills. It's a career move, and a good one. It's part of a succession plan almost as intimidating as the job itself, if I'm honest. It doesn't change the fact that if I could manage my career while staying here the entire time, I would. That's not how the Army works, though. So here we are.

I'm lost in thoughts of staffing and training when I hear the door behind me creak open and Megan sits beside me. Her hair is a matted mess on her head, with an elastic hanging off a few strands in the back. She's wearing an old PT shirt of mine, but even though it's too big for her, her tits stretch the fabric and I can see the wet mark of her nipples pressing against the logo. She's thrown on a pair of sweat shorts, the bright, pale skin of her upper thighs peeking out just below them before the line of where the capris she usually wears shows her slight tan. There's smudges under her eyes, when she bumps shoulders with me and smiles. My eyes linger on the fullness of her pink lips. I reach up and run my thumb across her bottom lip before giving her a quick kiss on the forehead, so I don't knock her over with what I'm sure is my morning coffee breath. She smells faintly like her fruity shampoo. I reach down and make a quick adjustment since these thin PJ pants hide nothing.

She stares wistfully out towards the street for a moment. "Remember when Tori managed to push the door open and crawled all the way to the neighbour's house before we even noticed she was gone?"

I blink at her a few times. "Um, what? That happened? How did that happen?"

She seems unconcerned. Why is she not concerned about this?

"Oh, were you not here? I guess not. Ya, it was hilarious. When I noticed the door open, I stepped out just when I heard

Michelle laughing next door. She had managed to crawl all the way around the hedge and up to her step!" Megan chuckles. This doesn't sound funny to me.

"Where were you? How old was she? I mean, she could have been..."

"I don't remember what I was doing. It could only have been a few minutes. Man, she was fast! Remember that?"

I bite my tongue that wants to admonish her for letting this happen years ago. It's too late now. I fail to see how that's funny, though. How does a baby sneak out of the house without being noticed? Megan doesn't notice my frustration, or if she does, she's gotten good at ignoring it. She's still smiling, staring off at nothing, remembering.

"I'm going to miss this place."

"Really? It's old and cramped. We're just lucky someone bought it quickly and the move has been pretty painless."

"Painless? You mean how I met a realtor and put it on the market while you were in the field? Or how I kept it spotless for showings on my own with two toddlers? I don't know that I'd describe taking down all those doors and repainting them during the kids' naptimes as painless."

I open my mouth but decide to just close it. I don't know if there's a good response to that. Sometimes I forget all those things at home don't just happen. I mean, it's not like I can worry about it while I'm in Wainwright.

"This is where we brought the kids home from the hospital. They both took their first steps here, said their first words. I know it's not the nicest place, but this is where we spent our first night together. I'll miss what made it our home."

I look over my shoulder at the screen door and into the front of the house, trying to see it through her eyes. All I see is the cracked hinge and the scuff marks on the wall from tiny shoes being kicked off. The new house is open, more room in the backyard for the kids to play. The kind of house I should be providing my family. I should have been providing all along. The very least I could do, since I'm never home with them, is give them all they could possibly need.

No, I can't bring myself to miss this place.

"I guess it will be an opportunity for Tori and Vince to learn the language, or at least be exposed to it. I really don't know if I'm going to find a job there. Every insurance agency I try anywhere near our place requires French."

My mind wanders to the French refresher I'll take when I arrive this summer. Though most of the Francophone troops are bilingual, I'll be expected to teach some in French. I really don't know how I'm going to pull it all off. Megan's been home on maternity leave; that will wrap up just as we're moving, but to be honest, cost of living there is a little lower and so is our new mortgage. I'm not that worried about Megan going back to work during our time there. We'll be fine and I'm sure she'll enjoy being home with the kids more.

I turn to her to say so when a commotion inside interrupts me.

"Mom. Mommy. Mommyyyyyyyy. Mommmyyyyyyyy! MOMMYYYYYYYYY!" Apparently, Tori is up and exactly point two seconds after her outburst, Vince's sharp cry comes from the same direction. Megan gets up with a sigh.

"All our stuff is packed, I have nothing to feed them," she calls to me as the screen door clatters behind her.

"McDonald's?" I call back.

"That's why I love you," she yells over the sound of Vince's howls as she changes him on top of a sealed box with Tori jumping on the air mattress behind her.

And just like that, we're moving on.

16

MEGAN

SPRING 2003

*H*is fitful tossing is always the first sign.

It takes me a moment to awake to it. I'm not as sensitive to all his fussing in his sleep anymore, it's been months and I've slowly gotten used to it... I think. I can immediately tell this isn't the kind that will let him settle again.

Sometimes, the dreams will let him go after a few minutes, but most of the time, they aren't happy until he's awake. One of the hardest lessons for me has been that there is nothing I can do to change them, or their intentions with him in the night.

When he starts mumbling, I prepare myself. I'm not even completely awake but it's become a routine to me. I'm pretty sure I do it in my sleep sometimes.

I can never quite make out what he's saying, though I have tried so many times. I'd love the chance to hear what's going on in his head, to know what it is that only seems to haunt him when he's resting. It never makes it out of his mouth in any more than mumbles and whispers.

When he starts searching with his hands, grabbing at the pillow and finally at me, I know he's reached the point where he's just starting to wake. If it was still dark out, I'd pass him a pillow, pretending it's what he wants, and hope he can settle, but the living room is bathed in light, so I just try to make his transition to the day as gentle as it can be.

"We're at home, Mark. Your rifle isn't here. Go back to sleep."

He stills for a moment, his hand holding my hip, and then he relaxes. He's awake. I roll back to the kids and settle again. Vince was up so often in the night, crammed on this mattress with the three of us, I'm exhausted. I hear Mark slide out of bed and grab a coffee, his feet almost soundlessly padding out the front door. Vince stirs a moment, so I turn his head towards me and stick a boob in his mouth until he settles back to sleep. Sleep isn't going to come again now, so once I'm sure I have a few moments where they'll both stay out, I slip out of the bed myself, fill up my mug, and follow Mark to the step.

For a moment, I watch him from behind. His shoulders are so strong, and the muscles in his back make me flutter. He just got his hair cut yesterday, the fade of the standard military look leading to his black hair, the same crazy dark shade the kids got. I follow the lines of his back to where his pants sit just above his ass, and I tamp down the desire to wrap myself around him from behind. It seems almost unfair how much more attractive Mark has become as we've been married. He's filled out and he moves with even that much more confidence. I, on the other hand, have turned into a cliché, an overweight mom of two, with all the stretch marks and sags to go along with it.

I sit next to him and rub up against his shoulder in hello. He looks over at me for a moment and I think he'll kiss me but instead, he just gives me a quick brush of his lips on my forehead. I guess I probably look even more of a fright than I thought. He shifts on the step and I take a second to run my fingers through my greasy hair and look down to see the wet marks from leaky boobs on his t-shirt.

No wonder he didn't kiss me. I must look like hell.

We sit quietly for a moment, and I smile at old memories that come back to me in this home. When I tell him the story of Victoria crawling down the sidewalk, I know it gets his back up but honestly, I don't really care that much. It happened years before and Mark doesn't get what being a solo parent looks like day to day. I'm pretty sure he thinks I do nothing but watch TV while the kids run wild.

I love this old house. That front entrance, it still reminds me of the night Mark led me through the front door and pinned me against the wall in our first kiss. There's a stain on the carpet from the time we were both figuring out how to change Victoria when she had pooped all the way up to her neck and somehow managed to drop the diaper shit side down on the floor. We both ended up on the floor with the diaper between us, laughing until we had tears, before we cleaned it and Tori up.

I'll miss the neighbours, and the comfort of familiar surroundings. Having Cheryl nearby. Being able to drive down and see my dad. This move will change so much on my day to day and now that we sit here on this very last day, it's all started to really hit me.

So, when Mark comments about the painless move, I may have reacted with a little venom. He just doesn't get all that I did, or all I'm giving up. For him. I'm moving for him. Leaving the job I had here, my family, my home.

I do it willingly. I'd follow him anywhere, but does he not see that it's not easy for me, either? I just want him to acknowledge what I'm giving up for him. Just once. I never wanted to be a stay-at-home mom. I love working and I enjoyed my job, but I don't know how I'm going to keep that up while I'm there. If I don't find a job, it will be just me and the kids. I might end up just losing my mind all day with them.

I'm lost in thoughts about fitting new curtains, job hunting, and how to make sure vaccinations stay on schedule while we look for a new doctor when I hear the familiar screech of the kids waking up looking for me. I head inside as Vince wails to eat, and throw a blanket on a box so I can change him.

I realize I have nothing in the fridge. Nothing. We probably should have thought this through. When I tell Mark, he doesn't skip a beat.

"McDonalds?"

At least, even with all the mess, we still make a good team.

And just like that, it's time to go.

17

MARK

PRESENT

I finally walk into battalion the next morning before visiting Megan. Since I all but ran here from Toronto when Matt emailed me, I'm not sure what the plan is anymore. I can't just go back to school at the staff college that I've been at these past months. I don't know when I will be able to, not when Megan is here and is this sick. It's not my choice, though, so I'm going to need to convince the ones whose choice it is that there's a way I can stay.

"Major Lawson? What are you doing back here? Visiting the family?" One of the young captains approaches me almost as soon as I make it in the front door. I should have planned this better. I don't want to talk to anyone I don't have to.

"Something like that." I give my best attempt at a smile, so I don't come across as too big a douchebag and keep moving. I'm hoping to see Lt. Col Patch and see where I might go from here while staying around Megan for the time being.

I barely make it up the stairs before I run right into him and he's quick to grab my shoulder and move us to his office.

"Mark. Come in, I have a minute now. Let's figure this out."

I've always appreciated the CO's bluntness, even in our younger days when he was my captain. The benefit of being around a while now is many of my command team are guys I've served with for years, both at home and overseas. It's easier to go to them in times I need to.

I've never needed to.

I never thought I needed to, anyways.

I guess now I do.

I walk into the corner office and over to the stiff couch against the far wall. I'm not in here all that often. That's a good thing. I take a deep breath and sit down while Lt. Col Patch moves a chair so he's in front of me.

"First off, how's Megan?"

"She's... Well, she's okay for now, sir. The infection is being managed and once it's under control, it looks like she can start chemo again. Doctors think in a few days she should be able to go home."

The CO nods before he gets up and looks down at some files on his desk. It's silent in his office for a moment but not uncomfortable. Lt. Col Patch is a man that only speaks if he knows something worthwhile to say.

"Breast cancer is a bitch. My mom fought twice before we lost her last year."

"I'm sorry to hear that, sir."

He nods once. "It was much closer to her time to go, though a shitty way to be taken out, I agree. Well, you need to be closer to her for the next while. That's a given. I'm going to do my best. Hopefully by the end of this week, we can get confirmation that you can finish school at a distance instead of the college in Toronto while we keep you nearby. It's above my paygrade though so I'm going to have to jump some hoops before I give you the green light."

"Sir, I don't want…"

"Look, Mark, you've never been the one in here with a hundred requests. Your wife having cancer is more than enough reason to consider a compassionate transfer." He stares at me a moment longer.

"I'm going to assume there was a reason you didn't say anything when the posting message came in six months ago?"

The words stick in my throat for a minute. I'm already swallowing my pride here. I might as well jump all in.

"I didn't know until this weekend, sir."

He blinks. "You two are still together?"

"Yes, sir."

Now one corner of his mouth pulls up slightly and he shakes his head slowly.

"That's quite the woman you got there."

"I'm here now, though, sir."

"That you are. We'll do our best to keep you around as long as we can, too. I think you've got more work cut out for you with her than cancer."

I shake his hand as I stand and leave his office.

Every single person I've spoken to since I've arrived seems to have more insight into my wife than I do.

A half hour later, I stand on Cheryl's porch to pick up Vince and Tori. There's a paper stuck over the doorbell warning people not to wake up any sleeping babies, so I just open the door without knocking. The inside is strangely quiet as Cheryl bounces Dylan on her hip.

"Oh, hi," Cheryl says when she turns and sees me. She's never been my biggest fan and it's looking more likely that this has pushed me over the edge from tolerated to openly despised. I decide to go with compliments and kindness. I don't need a new enemy right now.

"Hey. It's so quiet in here, I don't know how you do it." Cheryl wipes soapy hands from the sink on her jeans, smearing wet marks down her thighs. She gives me a curious look.

"Well, Dylan is the only one here. The rest are at school. Vince will be home from kindergarten at eleven forty-five though."

I stand there quiet for a moment. Of course, school. I'm an idiot. I do my best not to let my surprise show on my face; the last thing I need is to give Cheryl more ammunition in her campaign against me.

"You had no idea your kids were at school, did you?"

Shit, I guess I didn't hide it at all.

"Honestly, Cheryl, I barely even know what day it is," I offer an excuse. I've been trying to win this woman over for nine years, so I doubt it will work. She doesn't say anything, just drops Dylan down into an exer-saucer and walks back to the kitchen.

"Well, Vince will be home in less than an hour. You want a coffee while you wait?" The kitchen is a mess of mostly plastic dishes scattered along the counters and an open cupboard above the floor has Tupperware spilling out. Dylan bounces vigorously, as though he really believes he might get somewhere with the movement, all the while babbling to himself. I look up and catch Cheryl watching me again and realize I never answered her question.

"Um, you know what? If it's okay with you, I'll go visit Megan, and come back after school."

Cheryl seems to study me for a moment before nodding.

"Yup. Go ahead, you know where we'll be."

I consider saying more, but decide against it. I'm not going to win any battles here. Instead, I just walk out the door with a mumbled thanks.

When I get to Megan's room, she's sitting up flipping channels on the TV. She looks up at me when I walk in and flips the screen off, putting the remote down next to her before settling herself facing the direction of the lone chair in the room as I sit down. Her skin is a little less pale and her hair is pulled back from her face. She still has the heart monitor and IV in, but she has at least stopped looking like she's cheating death.

"Hey, Mark." Her voice is quiet, almost resigned. I have a thousand things I want to say, answers I want from her.

"I brought you a chai," I say lamely instead and set the Starbucks cup on the tray next to her uneaten breakfast.

"Thanks."

The silence grows between us like it's a physical thing pushing us apart.

"Megan..."

"Look, Mark..."

We both talk at once and she almost smiles. I lift my hand to her to continue first and for a second, I think she'll argue, but she keeps talking.

"I just didn't want to worry you when you were gone. That's all. I really am going to be okay." This time she does smile, a sad turn up of her mouth that changes nothing else on her face.

"Megan..."

"No, Mark, just listen. When you were in Afghanistan in the spring, we could barely talk, and it didn't seem like a big enough deal to have to let you know. And then when you were moving for school..."

Her unspoken words, the truth of it sits heavy in the room.

When I was moving.

When we broke apart.

"If I would have known, then..."

"Then what, Mark? It would have made things work better? It would have made *us* work better?"

"I don't know, Megan, but at least we would have been on the same page? I've been living my life for however long now, not knowing my wife is living hers with cancer!"

"And that way you could do your job!"

"YOU ARE MY JOB!"

The room seems even quieter after the loud roar of my response. I can hear the swooshing pump of the IV line that seems to match my ragged breath. Megan just watches me for a while.

"No. No, Mark. The Army is your job. Your men, your unit, the war… that's your job. Me, the kids, the house, that's all my job. That's how it's always been. Cancer doesn't magically change that."

I have nothing to say. I want to argue, to tell her she's being overly dramatic and it's never worked that way, but it would be a lie. I hate that I know that.

I look around, realizing I stood in my frustration, and I flop back down on the chair next to her bed, the room echoing with the scrape of the legs on the floor as my body weight pushes the whole thing back.

"Seven months."

I look up at her questioningly.

"That's when I found out. It's been seven months."

My head drops into my hands.

We've been broken so much longer than that.

18

MEGAN

SPRING 2005

I hate this place.
I hate the house and the school and the language and the driving and...

I don't mean any of that.

I'm just tired.

They say you'll just adapt and make friends when you are posted with the military but so far, I don't have an ear for French no matter how many times I attempt the classes and the online training, I haven't met anyone, and I feel like I'm stuck in a constant Groundhog Day loop of school drop offs and pick-ups and nights at home in front of the small selection of English TV.

I'd kill for any reason to get out of this house, but I gave up on the job front after six months when I didn't have one single prospect, even after dozens of resumes and even a few meetings with a local employment agency.

They recommended I "brush up" on my French language skills.

That assumed I had any to begin with.

So even now, two years after we arrived, Tori and Vince speak better French than I do, and I spend my days at home, or driving kids to and from school and playgroup.

I know being a stay-at-home mom is something many women dream of the opportunity for. It was never my dream and I feel guilty over how much I hate it most days. I should be grateful we can afford it and happy to spend the time with the kids. Instead, I just feel trapped, isolated, and angry. This is the exact replica of the life I tried to avoid when I left home.

I wanted to travel the world.

Instead, my husband does, and I stay home and watch the kids.

Vince babbles in the backseat now as we wait for Tori to come out in the pick-up line at her school. There's a dozen other moms on this same street, all of us staring at books or eyes closed, listening to music. None of us talking. We don't even get out of our cliché minivans.

Once the bell rings, it doesn't take long for Victoria's bouncing dark curls to break through the crowd and come running. I wish I had her enthusiasm for virtually everything. She's kept me sane, for all that I hate here she loves just as fiercely. She loves *everything*.

I get out and open the van door for her.

"Hey, princess, how was your day?" She hugs my legs before jumping in, tossing her backpack on the floor with a thud.

"The best! Miss Gagne taught us TWO new songs. I'm going to sing them for you and Daddy tonight! Can I? Oooooooh, I really want to sing them! I'll start now so I don't forget them before Dad gets home…"

As usual, she's talking a mile a minute and I can barely keep up. I just interject with little "mhmm," every once and a while when she comes up for breath. Soon, she's singing in French to her captive backseat audience of one. Vince, at least, doesn't seem perturbed.

It's not too long before we pull into our place. The brick bungalow with the sprawling yard is gorgeous and if nothing else, the highlight of our time here. The gorgeous maple trees stand tall in front like they're a last line of defence before the wraparound porch. Pulling into the garage, we walk out into the backyard where the kids have more toys than twenty kids would need sprawled everywhere. They both get distracted by one which is fine by me as I head in the back to get dinner ready.

My kitchen here is lovely; the last owners cut out some walls and the entire space is open and bright. This, however, doesn't make me any more domestic. I open the fridge and stare inside as though it is hiding the secret of what I'm going to pull out for dinner like I had something planned all day. Absently, I grab what I need for a big salad and open the freezer for some chicken, tossing a handful of seasoning on top of the still-frozen breasts and sticking them in the heating oven. I'll cook up some frozen pasta and there. Dinner is done for another day.

That hardly feels like an accomplishment when I know they're just going to want something again tomorrow.

Like I said. You can bring the girl to the kitchen…

While I cut the veggies, I hear the shriek of the kids letting me know Mark must be home. A few moments later, the back door opens and he's in, dumping his massive bag on the floor before plopping down on the entrance step to take off his boots.

"Hey, babe," I call from where I'm standing at the counter. He grunts in response.

Lovely.

I hear the loud thunk of his boots that lets me know they

definitely hit the door before falling to the floor and then he's behind me, hand on my hip and lips in my hair, giving me a quick kiss on the top of my head before he saunters off to the bedroom to change.

"Want to go to a party this weekend?" he calls to me from other room.

"What? You mean in two days?"

He can't be serious.

"Ya!" His voice gets closer as he comes back into the kitchen; now he's in faded jeans and the green combat shirt from under his uniform. The shirt is faded, threadbare under the arms and too small. Even though it's been almost seven years, I still linger a moment on him, the way he takes over the room just by being in it, the way his shirt only highlights his strong shoulders and biceps, and the Canadian flag tattoo that peeks out from the sleeve.

He leans against the fridge and crosses his arms, his eyes watching me flit around the small space as I finish pulling dinner together.

"There's a dinner at the Officer's Mess on Saturday. I forgot to mention it. I have to be there, you should come!"

I stand in front of him, a tray of chicken from the oven in my hands, and blink for a few moments before I turn away to put it on the counter and pull out the plates.

"And what would I do with the kids?"

"I dunno, hire a sitter?"

I sigh loudly and overly dramatically while I plate the food from the counter and move it over to the table. He's still leaning against the fridge.

"What? That's what people do, Meg. They hire sitters and go out!"

"I get that, but where will I find this sitter? We don't know anyone and it's only a couple days' notice. How would I find someone to meet and get to know the kids before then?"

FIGHT FOR HOME

Mark finally moves, scooping Vince up off the couch and onto his booster seat at the table, with Tori following closely behind and jumping into her seat. Mark and I both sit in front of our food and Tori starts into her stories about teachers and songs while Vince starts throwing his chicken into the centerpiece.

Talk of parties will have to wait.

After thirteen books and listening to several renditions of francophone preschool songs, both kids are tucked into bed and I finally click Tori's door behind me as I see Mark leaving Vince's room down the hall. He grabs a bottle of Keith's from the fridge about the same time I head to the dining room with a corkscrew and a glass for a generous pour of some cheap red. By the time we both plop ourselves in front of the TV in the living room, I've all but forgotten our conversation earlier.

"So…" Mark starts as he picks at the label on his beer bottle.

"Dinner is at six thirty. It's not an option for me to be there. All the instructors need to go. You don't have to come if you don't want to."

"It's not that I don't want to. I just don't see how I can pull that together. We've been here almost two years and I haven't found a sitter yet. I doubt I'm going to scrounge one up on two days' notice. It's fine, go have fun."

Since we've moved here, Mark has settled into a routine. He's home most nights, which is a change from battalion, but the constant cycle of classes and instructors has him busy during the day and while I know he misses his unit, he has found a few other infantry officers like him that he's enjoyed spending his free time with.

None of them are married, so it never includes me.

That's fine, I have the kids at home anyways.

The longer we're here, the more talk revolves around succession plans and who's going where, and where he needs to be that would be best for him and his career. It's all about career progression and we factor in less and less every year.

He looks at me like he doesn't believe me, which is probably smart on his part. I don't feel like having an argument over it. It can't be fixed now. I try to lighten the mood.

"When we get back to Edmonton this summer, we can leave the kids with Cheryl and go on dates again."

Mark immediately diverts his eyes.

Oh no.

Oh HELL no.

"Mark. We ARE leaving this summer, right?"

"The thing is, babe, the spot I was going to move into isn't open yet. It doesn't make sense to bring me back to battalion without it, so…"

You have gotta be shitting me.

"No. You don't understand. I have spent every moment here looking forward to leaving back home. Now you're telling me you're adding another year to my sentence as though it's not a big deal!"

I've scooted back from him on the couch, twisting around so I can see him face to face, but he's not turning, staring straight ahead at the TV and still picking at the label of the damn bottle.

"It's just another year, Meg. One year. We won't be here forever…"

"THAT'S WHAT YOU SAID WHEN YOU BROUGHT ME HERE."

"Meg, you're going to wake up the kids."

Is he serious right now?

"You need to tell them I want to go back now. NOW. This isn't fair, Mark! You said two years!"

I take a moment, our breath between us filling the quiet, before I down the rest of my wine in one gulp and head back to the dining room, pouring double the generous amount I poured the first time. He quirks a brow at me, but I stare him down.

He says nothing. He knows I didn't mean it. I never do. I just needed to get it out. I'm not done being mad, though. Not by a long shot.

"I'm taking a bath."

It's a statement and it leaves no room for comment. The door to the bathroom slams behind me and the tears start almost immediately. I run the water to hide the sound and strip down, avoiding looking in the mirror at the road map of sags and stretch marks that cover what was never a supermodel body to begin with. No sense in adding insult to injury tonight.

Under the water, I close my eyes and let the sound of the still filling tub fill my ears as most of my head is under the suds. I give myself time. I just need time. I'm stronger than this hissy fit I just threw.

I miss my sister, and my dad. I miss working, I miss friends, I miss all-English TV.

It hasn't all been bad, though. Mark is home more often. The kids are happy. The house is beautiful.

Ugh.

I'm such a drama queen. This is just another year. Just a bump in the road, not the end of the world. Hundreds, thousands of other military wives have managed this life before me, it can be done.

I can do this.

I just need a minute.

Once my wine is done, I take a few final deep breaths and pull myself out of the tub, drying off quickly and not even bothering with getting dressed again. I walk into the bedroom in my towel where Mark lies in bed looking over some papers. He looks up immediately, hooded eyes following my figure as I step over to my side of the bed.

I sit on the side before I drop the towel and pull the covers over me in almost one smooth motion. I hear a frustrated sigh behind me.

There's no way he wants to see that jiggle with the lights on, as much as he thinks he might.

I hear him put the papers down and click off the light before I feel his lips on the side of my throat. There's goosebumps up my arms as he kisses me softly up the curve of my neck and up to my jaw. I'm about ready to pull away and ignore his advances for sleep, but his hand teases as it travels down my side; the warmth feels nice and I find myself unexpectedly willing.

Damn him.

I stiffen as it reaches my stomach, but he never stalls in his exploration, even when I feel his hands trail the curve of my belly, the sags in my skin, and the bumped texture of my stretch marks. When he cups my breast with his hand and gently flicks his fingers over the sensitive peak, I give in and turn over into him.

He takes me reverently at first, like an apology. That's not where he stops, though. He never could keep up that slow a pace and he knows that's not what I want, either.

After all these years getting comfortable together, it's like he can play my body like an instrument. He once told me since he couldn't play a note, it was more like he knew me like he knows a rifle. He can take me apart with his eyes closed. He takes my hands in his when he slips over top of me and drags them above my head, taking them both in one of his before using his other hand to tease me while he rocks his body into me, hard, over and over until neither of us feels anything else. Until we start to make sense again.

When we both finally fall apart, he drops his head into my neck, the sweat from the effort making his face slide on my skin, his breath coming in loud pants in my ear. I close my eyes at the feel of him, the smell, the warmth. All too soon, he rolls to the side and we clean ourselves in silence. When he lies back down, he's too far away.

"I'm sorry," he whispers out to the silence. I'm not even sure what part of all of this it is he's sorry about, but I have no doubt he means it nonetheless. I do too.

"I know," I say back, and I soon hear his breathing even out.

What I don't say is I just don't know anymore if that's always going to be enough.

19

MARK

FALL 2005

*P*iecing together my dress uniform here always seems out of place.

The tailor doesn't see my patches all that often, and I have yet to meet another Afghanistan veteran at this base.

Instead, it's instructors pieced together from all over the country, which is great, but there are some days I miss battalion more than others and this is one of them. I'm always being asked to talk at some school or stand at some parade for the weeks leading up to it. This year, I'm headed to Victoria's school's ceremony because it's not a stat holiday and I don't know if I'll ever get used to the kids having class on this day.

I've been standing close to an hour in front of this uniform as it hangs in the doorway, trying to line up my medals and that pin that goes on my pocket just below. All of it means so little to me and there's not much that is more important. No one here will say a word if it is crooked, but I'll know.

"Vince, get back here!" I hear a high-pitched giggle. I assume the little blonde-haired, blue-eyed con artist managed to evade his mother's grasp again as she's out in the living room getting them ready. This is confirmed by the sound of her tearing down the hallway, chasing his squeals.

These ceremonies take on a whole different aspect when I spend them here with family. Try explaining to a three and five-year-old that it's a solemn occasion.

It doesn't go over well.

I know because we tried all week.

I finally give my jacket one more go-over with the lint brush and pull it on over the pants and green dress shirt and tie I was already wearing, and head out into the hall. Megan wrestles something on Vince and I see Tori sitting nicely by the door. That's my girl.

At least she's listening. She's sitting there so nice and quiet, her black hair curled around her smiling face with the cutest dimples, the crinoline of her red dress billowing around her. She's just playing with something in her lap, waiting to leave. Whatever toy she's got is black and shiny. Wait, is it on her hands too?

Holy.

Hell.

Those.

Are.

My.

Shoes.

It takes about three strides for me to make it over to her. There's polish from the little jar I had sitting in my kit next to the boots, all over her hands and one of my dress boots. She's drawing on the toe with her fingers, the black smearing into the finish and onto her dress.

"Victoria! No! No! What were you thinking! No!" I grab her and stand her up, the shoe falling onto the floor, toe first of course. With a hand on her back, I march her to the kitchen.

"Don't move." She just looks up at me, her little lip quivering as she stares at my axe hand in her face.

"I just make them shiny!"

"You know you can't touch my Army things, Victoria! Now stand there and don't touch anything!"

I sprint back to the entrance and grab my shoes. She's only gotten to the one, but it's destroyed. I look at my watch. I have less than twenty minutes before we need to be at the school.

"MEGAN!" I bellow as I pull my jacket back off, smoothing it back on a hanger off the front of the closet doorknob and grabbing the shine brush from my kit bag that's spilt all over the floor.

"MEGAN!"

Megan comes in from the hall, a newly dressed Vince on her hip.

"What, Mark?" Her tone is clipped and tired.

"Deal with Victoria please."

Megan sets Vince down and he immediately starts a beeline for my direction. I put a protective arm out.

"Sorry, buddy, you need to stay over there."

He keeps trying, attempting to duck under the arm I have out while I try to use the other hand to buff down the mess of polish Tori has left.

"Vince, I said no!"

Vince plops down on his diapered ass with a loud thump and wails.

"MEGAN!"

I can hear Megan and Victoria chatting in the kitchen along with the sound of running water, and Megan pokes her head around the corner.

"Kinda busy." Victoria darts from behind her, butt ass naked, and streaks to her room.

"Your blue dress with the yellow. And don't forget panties!" Megan calls after her.

"Okay, you're busy, but you need to deal with Vince. My boots aren't going to be fixed in time as it is."

Megan gives a loud sigh and walks over to where Vince is still wailing on the ground next to me, scooping him up with one arm while drying her other hand on a dishcloth. The black pants and sweater that she's wearing already have smears on them at kid height, her hair falling out in every direction from the bun she had it in.

"I got him."

She carries him like a football back to the kitchen where I hear her running more water. I have no idea what the hell she's doing until I see her emerge, still holding Vince, with Tori's dress soaked and smeared with soap before she throws it down to the laundry room.

Huh. I never would have thought of that.

Megan takes Vince in with her to check on Victoria and I finally think the shoes are as good as they're gonna get. Fuck, I hate going out looking less than 100%, especially today, but I don't have any choice. We need to be at the ceremony now.

"Let's GO!" I grab the keys and head to the car, opening the garage and gingerly getting myself behind the wheel. It feels like forever before I finally see the door open and Victoria is in her new dress. Vince is in his dress shirt and tie, and Megan looks more than a little dishevelled.

"Meg, you're going to fix your hair before we get in there, right?" Right now, her face is red, and her hair is in every direction except back where she put it. She looks back at me from where she's buckling in Vince, her eyes scowl and her mouth presses into a small line.

"Fine, never mind." Once the kids are settled, I take off like a shot. I can't be late for this. I can't. Remembrance Day isn't the day to try out what it's like not to show up on time.

The entire school ceremony takes less than half an hour. Everyone thanks me for my service as though I'm the one that died. If I must smile awkwardly one more time while someone shakes my hand and asks if I've seen any 'action,' I might bite my tongue clean the fuck off.

I need to get away from these people.

The drive back home is quiet, Tori softly hums the last post from the backseat and I must remind myself over and over that she's not trying to make me mad, she's just being a little girl. I'm close to losing it on all of them and I know it's not fair. I need to go.

When I pull in the driveway, I open the garage door and park, not getting out. Megan looks at me questioningly while she unbuckles Vince from his car seat.

"I'm going to the Legion."

She opens her mouth but closes it quickly and nods. She and the kids disappear in the house. I pull out and take off before I can feel bad about it and head to meet some of the guys. I've met a few other infantry officers here and when I walk in, they're hanging at the bar, like I thought they might be. I grab a beer and sit with them, but even there, it's mostly quiet. They weren't there. They don't have the same memories, they aren't here for the same reason.

They don't remember the same war.

Their head isn't filled with the voices of the same people.

We trade stories for a while, try to lighten the mood. The other soldiers and veterans here are all rambunctious, getting louder by the minute as they keep drinking. The cynical part of me wants to turn and ask them how they think they deserve the free dinners and coffee and drinks they've been bought all day, when they've never once fired in anger. That's not fair, though. Truth be told, I'd bet they'd all wished with all they were they could have been where I was. Probably would until that moment when they didn't. Just like me.

They're all having a good time, but I can't seem to fit in. When my phone rings in my pocket, I assume it's Megan and I almost ignore it, only because selfishly I know I'm drunk and I don't want to feel guilty.

I head outside instead though to answer, and I'm surprised when I hear Dennis' voice on the other end.

"Hey, man."

I haven't heard from him in almost a year. He went to New Brunswick when I came here and neither of us are the best at communication.

"Hey. How's things?"

His voice is slurred, even more so than mine, and his words are slow in coming.

"I jus needed to talk to summun who was there, yaknow?"

His breath comes heavy over the line.

"I get it, man. Where are you?"

"My room. Same kinna room I had when I was a subbie, nothin really changes, hey?"

I give a stilted laugh at the mention of the crappy rooms we had on base, a shared bathroom between us, back when we were sub lieutenants.

"You alone?"

"Always."

Fuck.

"Hey, look, why don't you cab it to the Legion or something, hey? See some of the guys there?"

"Immin no shape fer that. 'Sides, there's noone, you know? There's guys, but there's not any *guys* here."

"There's me. I'm glad you called."

"Ya. Hey, remember when we were in Guam and we woke up the captain by throwing that dried scorpion from the shadow box on his face?"

He chuckles, a raspy sound that ends abruptly with the sound of him taking another drink. I take a deep breath and give a little laugh.

"I do, screamed like a little girl."

FIGHT FOR HOME

There's silence on the line for a long time. We're both lost in our thoughts. Weirdly, even though we aren't saying anything, it feels nice to be lost in them together.

"Anyways, man, thanks for picking up the phone. I think I'm gonna crash, a'ite?"

"Ya. Ya, okay. Thanks for calling, Dennis."

"Sure."

The line goes dead before I can even take the phone from my ear.

I probably should have asked him if he was really okay.

Instead, I just call a cab and head home alone. When I finally pull off my uniform and crawl into bed, Megan only barely stirs.

"Hey, baby," she mumbles into the pillow. She blinks a few times before looking at me.

"Everything okay?"

Her hair is still damp; she probably used the chance for a shower once she got the kids in bed. There's a line down her cheek from the pillow crease, and her eyes are hooded with sleep.

I can't believe she puts up with this. With me. In this province with both kids, while I run off and drink with strangers while she keeps the kids and house. The room spins a little as I watch the rise and fall of her chest, the thin, stretched straps of the tank top she has on have fallen down both arms. I can clearly see the outline of each breast through the worn fabric, and my body stirs.

It probably makes me the worst husband, but I'm going to take this.

I need her.

"I'm right here," she whispers. I hadn't realized I'd said that last part aloud. Instead of answering, I brush her shirt the rest of the way down until she's exposed to me, the chilled air hitting her, leaving goosebumps on her soft skin. I look at her face and while it doesn't look as eager as I hoped, she's not pushing me away, either. These days, that's a win and I'll run with it.

I lower my head and devour her for a moment until I hear the softest moan. That's what I was looking for. Sitting back, I kiss her full mouth gently before rolling her over onto her stomach, throwing a knee over her legs until I'm sitting over her, and running my hands firmly down her sides. I know I have her when her back instinctively arches, pushing her ass up against me. I take her in one motion and bask in the startled cry from her lips.

Wrapping my hands around the top of her full thighs, I push faster, letting one hand drift to hers where I move it over between her legs and she takes over, pushing back against me harder as she brings herself off.

I let the familiar feel of her body clear my head, until all I can think about is the space between us. The sweat drips down my back and my movements are jerky and desperate. There's no finesse, only the sounds of our bodies slapping together and the soft cries she buries in the mattress. It's only by sheer luck she finds her release moments before I feel myself lose it inside her.

I don't even grab her a cloth after. She tries to get up to the washroom to clean herself up, but I roll off on my side and grab her by the waist, pulling her against me and holding her there like she's the teddy bear I need to get to sleep. It takes no time at all for the exhaustion and the alcohol to claim my head and I drift off, my head buried in her hair, holding on for my life.

20

MEGAN

SPRING 2006

"*D*ad's gone."

The silence on the phone stretches and I find myself sitting down on the floor I just finished cleaning for the real estate photos tomorrow morning.

Two words and I'm an orphan.

I open my mouth three or four times before I croak out a response, "Daddy."

I hear Cheryl gulp back her own sobs. "They think it was a heart attack. One of his friends went to pick him up for a golf game and could see him on the floor through the window. The ambulance came and busted the door with the police. He was already gone." Her voice cracks and she dissolves back into tears.

I'm not sure why I'm not crying yet, but I'm not speaking, either. I've only seen my dad once in the three years we've been here. He flew out to visit last Christmas. He was strong, happy. Spoiled the kids and drove up to Quebec City with us.

We never visited there, though. Never found the extra money, or the time. Kept saying it was only a few years and we'd see him all the time again when we lived closer.

Only a few years.

We had lots of time.

"Daddy…"

"Hey, Megan." Paul's voice is gentle on the line. Cheryl must have passed the phone over. Or maybe he just took it when Cheryl couldn't speak.

"I'm so sorry." His voice is hoarse. He and my dad were close, they would fish together on long weekends. Paul had just spent a couple days there rebuilding my dad's deck. Mark and I were never there for that kind of thing. Not when we were away and not even when we were home. Mark was just gone so often, so we were so selfish with his time home with us.

Now, we had no time left at all.

"What… What's next?" I ask. I try to make myself think logically, all the things that needed to be done when Mom passed. I can't seem to make my brain work, though. Where's Mark? He will be able to help. I don't know where he went, though. He was talking on his Blackberry outside, last I saw him.

"Megan and I are just waiting for my parents to come over to watch the kids and then we'll head down there. I'm sure we'll have to plan a service, and deal with the condo. Cheryl hasn't thought that far ahead but I am here, and I can help…"

"I'll be there as soon as I can," I say it before I really think it through. I have no idea how I'll pull it off, or what we'll do with the kids, but I'm going to be there. I must be there. I'll figure it out.

I say a few more completely useless words to Paul and hang up. When Mark comes back in the room, I'm sitting on the stool that we have for the kids, staring at the phone in my hands.

"Meg, I have to… What's up?"

When I see him, the tears come. "Dad. He's… He's…" I can't

finish. I'm not even crying, just gasping for words and Mark stares for a moment before he gathers me up in his arms.

"Oh, Meg... I'm so sorry. Oh, Doll..." He continues to whisper in my ear while he pets my hair and holds me close to him. I lose myself in him for a moment, his warmth and the way his body can cover mine. I wish I had the luxury of staying lost there forever.

"I have to go home."

I hear his intake of breath and I know. This won't be easy. There's the kids, his job, the money for flights. It's not cheap and it's not something we have planned for. No one ever plans for this. I'm not even thirty yet.

"We'll make it work, doll. Just tell me what you need."

The rest of the night is a blur. Booking a flight out of Montreal, Mark calls Paul back so he knows when to pick me up. They talk for a while; it always makes me happy to see them get along but tonight I can't even think of that. I can't think of anything. By the time Mark puts me to bed a couple hours later, telling me he'll wake me for my flight in the morning, I don't feel anything at all. I don't know if Mark ever came to bed, but I'm grateful my bag is packed for me when Mark gently rustles me awake with coffee in the early hours before we head out the door.

When I get off the plane, I mindlessly make my way to the escalators. At the bottom of the stairs, Paul waits for me. Cheryl is still in bed, and that doesn't surprise me. I have the hour before I get to their place to be ready to be the big sister I'm supposed to be. I am the one that needs to take control, needs to make the decisions, and be ready to face the day. That's what my family deserves, especially after two and a half years without me.

Days there pass in a blur. Morgue. Funeral home. Cleaning. Planning.

Cheryl and I spend days in the house, packing. It's both the best and worst thing we have ever done, putting all my father had into boxes.

"Remember when Mom asked us to put some of our stuff aside to donate and we went into her room and filled a bag with clothes from her closet instead?"

Cheryl chuckles. "She searched the house for that ugly fuchsia skirt suit for weeks! We did her a favour, really. Who knows how long she might have kept wearing that thing."

We're knee deep in bags of Dad's old clothes. The smell of him, Old Spice cologne mixed with the musty scent of cheap cigars and the potpourri sachets Mom always kept in the clothing drawers, fills the room as we dig out his old sweater vests and golf shirts, throwing most in the bags going to charity. This part is easier than the photos and mementos he kept on the bedside table that we split up earlier. There's been a lot of tears this week, but we're getting through it.

It's just Cheryl and me here now. Paul took the kids back to Edmonton with him. We've been sleeping together in the guest bed here at Dad's condo, neither of us willing to take his bed. Instead, we huddle together, staying up talking into early morning some nights like we used to when we were kids and she would sneak into my room when the thunder woke her up. Telling each other stories of growing up. It's always funny to hear your memories retold by someone else, to hear another perspective to how things were.

One would think those times would be when the tears come, but it's not. Instead, it's the happiest time, remembering the love and laughter of what was overall a pretty idyllic childhood. The sadness doesn't come until we finish talking and the silence fills with the memories of how quickly I ran from it when I grew up, of all the missed visits after Mom died when I was 'too busy.' All those phone calls I told him I'd come 'next time.'

I want to blame the Army for this, for taking the last couple years from us, but if I'm honest with myself, I'd left way before that, before I'd even met Mark, and the visits had been few and far between even when I was only a couple hours away.

The Army makes an easier target, though.

Dad's bedroom is the last to pack, and we're almost done. Tomorrow, we have a truck coming from a local charity thrift store and they'll take most of these things away. When the last bag is closed, Cheryl looks over at me and smiles.

"Looks like we're all done."

We sit in silence for a long moment. We're done. This happened so fast, one phone call a couple days ago and now, it's already almost over, as though we should just move on now and forget. Soon, the condo will be empty and the day after tomorrow, the service will be over, too. It will be time to go back to our lives and a new normal. We're sisters without parents.

Does that make us orphans?

This whole week, Cheryl and I have been leaning on each other, but I look forward to getting back to Mark and letting all this go. So many decisions, everything clouded by emotions and grief, I miss my best friend and I just want to crawl under his arm and rest for a while.

The shrill ring of my new cell phone brings us both back to reality. It's Mark.

All I can think about is how good it's going to feel when I'm home and I can disappear, wrapped up in him. Close my eyes and let him hold me until it hurts less.

I've been craving that feeling since I arrived here.

"Hey, doll, how are things."

"Things suck." His voice is soft, but I'm irritated already, for no real reason other than the day's been shit and I need someone to really know that. I hear Victoria's squeal in the background.

"Mark, it's almost ten o'clock there. Why is Tori still awake?"

"It's fine, Megan. I can handle my own kids! I just needed to know when your dad's service is."

His voice is tense. I've already told him all this last night, so I immediately know something is up.

"It's Wednesday. Why?" He ignores my questions. This can't be good.

"So, do you plan on flying back Thursday?"

"I. Don't. Know. Why, Mark?"

"Our posting message came." Seriously, that's what he's worried about? That's the best news I've heard all week. Maybe all year.

"Really? Really?? Wait, it's for Edmonton, right?"

"Ya, Meg, it's for Edmonton. I'm going to be officer in command of a Charlie Company. It's just that... I need to take over the company earlier than expected."

"How much earlier?"

"I leave next week to go on exercise with them. After that... I'll probably stay, and you guys can join me when school is out."

I let the line sit silent for a minute, our breathing the only sound.

"Okay. When do you need me home?"

"Hopefully by the end of the week so I can pack up before I leave Monday."

I'll have to leave the day after the service, but it's okay. We're almost done here. And if we're moving back closer, I can help more this summer. Cheryl will understand.

I hope.

"Fine. I'll book my flight for Friday and I'll let you know when I come in. Could you call the realtor and get started with that?"

"I'll do my best, Meg, but I'm kind of trying to get the hand over done really quickly too, and I have the kids here."

Oh, he has the kids. Well, of course he can't do anything then. How could I *possibly* expect him to get anything done if he has the *kids*.

Sigh.

"Why the rush?"

"It's... it's just all the deployments and things, babe. They need people at battalion to manage it all."

"Are you deploying?"

"I'm not thinking that far ahead, Meg. Let's just get us all there, okay?"

"Sure, ya, okay. I... uh... I guess I'll see you on Friday. I better go and make sure I get everything wrapped up here."

"Okay, Meg. I love you, you know."

"I love you."

When I flip the phone shut, I just stare at it a moment. Cheryl stands in the doorway.

"You deserve more than this, Meg."

"It's not his fault, Cheryl."

"Right. It's never his fault. That doesn't make it easier, does it?"

I stand up off the floor and take a deep breath before I look up at her and smile.

"Let's find somewhere that serves wine, shall we?"

21

MEGAN

SUMMER 2006

I'm probably on my last nerve already when I hear the noise of the garage door opening over the sound of Toopy and Bino on the TV. Vince sits mindlessly on the carpet, surrounded by the mounds of toys he never bothers to even pretend to play with for our benefit. Victoria is up on the counter, colouring. I threw some sauce in a pot earlier so that's simmering on the stove, and I take the moment to try to kick as many toys as I can into a corner, so the place looks less like the children live here alone before Mark walks in.

It's been a... day. Between trying to find where the damn unpackers put the step stool for the kitchen, so I can put things away on the top shelves of the cupboard and trying to take all the photos of the crap the movers broke so I can send in a claim, I've had a four-year-old that wants to go back "home" and a seven-year-old that seems hell bent on finding new and unusual ways to make me lose my mind.

Her latest was to dig nail polish out of one of the still packed boxes in the bathroom and use it to 'decorate' the shower door.

I don't think I can convince my SIRVA claim that it happened during the move.

We still have only unpacked about half the boxes we told the unpackers to leave last week when we arrived. I was sick of them in my space, and any flat surface doesn't help me. Since I was convinced my bedding, towels, toiletries, and whatever those other miscellaneous boxes were probably weren't broken, I told them to just go.

Now I'm wondering how many of those boxes I will hide in the garage until the next move.

By the time the door from the garage opens, Vince has lost interest in the high-pitched squeals of the gender-confused rat, and he's made his way over to where his dad is coming in. I hear Mark toss his backpack on the ground before the familiar thud of his ass hitting the top stair while he takes his boots off. There's the smack of the boots hitting the door and falling to the ground.

Lovely.

"I seem to have some strange creature attached to me." He stands and Vince keeps his arms around his shoulders, hanging on like a monkey as Mark makes his way into the kitchen with big steps like a giant. I see him from the corner of my eye as he flinches while Vince screeches in his ear with laughter. He quickly sets him down on top of the kitchen table, and gives me a quick peck on the top of the head, ignoring the look I give him as I walk by to put Vince down on the floor.

Four-year-olds can't go on top of kitchen tables.

I thought that was common sense.

When I catch Mark's eye, though, he hasn't even registered my look and I see more than just weary, home from work stress in them. He's nervous, looking back and forth between me and the kids. Nervous has never been a good look on him, and I'm pretty sure there's very few things that can put that look on his face and most of them involve having to tell me something I don't want to hear.

Victoria has her arms out to him from the stool at the counter and he gives her a squeeze, but his eyes stay on me.

Dammit. This won't be good news.

I glance over at the wine bottle sitting by the sink. It's still half full, thankfully, since he looks like I need a drink.

"So, Meg..."

"Just spit it out, Mark."

He lets out a big sigh. "Charlie Company is officially headed to Afghanistan."

I blink a few times.

"What does that *mean*, Mark?"

"It means I'm deploying."

I stare at him a moment until the sauce on the counter decides to blow a gigantic bubble, spraying sauce on the stove. I run over, almost tripping over Vince who then decides to attach himself to my leg as I pull the pot off the burner and frantically wipe a wet cloth on the cooktop before the red liquid burns. I don't even turn around

"When?"

"Next month."

I swear I don't mean to throw the sauce-covered spoon.

There it goes, though, flying at his words, hitting the front of his uniform and spraying red on the wall, his epaulet, and his face before clattering to the floor.

He doesn't move. Vince whimpers so I pull him onto a hip, turn around, and continue to wipe the stove and counter. I'm wiping the same spot, over and over, jostling poor Vince on my side with such force I'm sure he regrets wanting up in the first place. I finally just put the cloth and Vince down, resting my hand on the counter and closing my eyes a moment.

Soon, I feel Mark's presence behind me. I hear Vince toddle

off towards the TV again. Mark's breath is in my ear and one hand comes from behind. I hear the tap of the spoon being put back onto the counter and his hands find purchase on my hips. I keep my eyes closed.

"We've got this."

I breathe through the burn I feel in my nose that threatens to fill my eyes with tears and reopen my eyes.

"I need to put water on for the spaghetti," I manage to get out. Mark uses my hips to spin me around to face him. The splash marks from where the spoon struck him look like a mini explosion coming from the middle of his chest. When I risk a glimpse at his eyes, I see a drop of sauce clinging to one of his eyelashes. I put my hand up slowly and he closes his eyes. I use the pad of my thumb to wipe his lash clean. When he opens again, his eyes search mine, so I look away.

"The spaghetti can wait, Meg."

"No, it can't. The sauce is getting cold." I twist from his arms and reach up to the big pot hanging from the ceiling above the island counter where Victoria is still obliviously colouring.

"Megan..."

"We have to eat, Mark. Unless, what? Are you leaving before dinner?"

"No. Meg..."

His words hang between us, but I just look over at him and paste on the sincerest fake smile I can muster, knowing I'm not fooling him for one damn minute. He stares at me a moment before he heads up the stairs. I assume to get himself changed.

We've got this.

I hate the phrase.

22

MARK

SUMMER 2006

*P*ulling my combats off, I ball them up and throw them to the landing of the stairs. I'll need to wash them by morning and tripping over them on my way back down is probably the best reminder I can give myself.

Not that I'm looking forward to heading back downstairs.

I knew Meg would be mad. Hell, we just got here. I know that, I do, and I'm not trying to be an asshole, but this is just the way it worked out. My brothers at battalion, they've been more than pulling their weight in this war, and it's time I got back out there and helped them.

I could have given her more of a head's up, but honestly, with her dad and then the move and all of it, I just never thought there was a good time. So, I waited until I was sure. It was the right choice, it doesn't do any good to have both of us worrying about something that might never happen.

At least that's how it looked from my side until right now, seeing how badly it went when I just caught her out of left field with it. I thought I was saving her some worry, but now I'm not sure that is better than this.

Either way, I'll just keep all that to myself. Can't change things now.

I'm just zipping up my jeans when Victoria comes bursting into our room. She's wearing multipattern leggings with what looks like the oldest tank top in existence overtop. It's got a huge stain on the front and the lace at the neckline is ripped. She has a glove on one hand, two different socks on, and her hair looks like it lost a fight with a bat.

So, she looks like it's Tuesday.

This girl cannot be tamed. Just the way I love her. She could probably use a hair elastic, though.

"Daddy! Daddy! Look! I drew you! Do you like it? Do you? I drew it!" She waves a paper about a half inch from my nose as though that will help me see anything. So far, all I see is that I'm very close to getting a papercut on my eyeball.

"Hey, relax, sweetie. I can't see it when you do that. Let me hold onto it and look." I take the paper from her eager hands. On it, there's a stick man with a green shirt and hat holding what I'm guessing is a gun. There's people on the ground. I think they might be dead.

"Um... what's going on here, Tori?"

"That's you, Daddy! That's you at work and those are the dead bad guys. Bang, bang!"

I look at the picture again. She's drawn so much detail in the flowers, the grass, the sky, the birds. And there's me, alone, surrounded by dead people.

"Victoria, you probably shouldn't be drawing people dying."

"Why not? Isn't that your job?"

I have no idea how to answer that. How do you explain war, or peacekeeping, or rules of engagement to a seven-year-old? Where did she even get these ideas?

I have the urge to lock her in a room and keep her innocent

forever, away from anyone that wants to teach her about how ugly the world is. Not for the first time.

"Well, it's not all I do, honey. Most of what I do is to help people. Protect people."

"Who are you protecting when you're far away?"

Victoria isn't old enough to remember my deployments, not really. She was a newborn, and then she was just a toddler. She'll remember this one, though. She'll have questions and fears that she was never old enough to experience before.

I'm not at all prepared for that.

"Well, I guess people like you, sweetie. If I can help people in other countries, and protect the kids there, then the bad guys don't come here. So, I'm protecting them and you at the same time."

This seems to be enough for her for now, and she smiles before running back downstairs, her hair bouncing behind her like it's a whole separate entity to itself. I watch her for a long time until the sound of her scampering feet fades when she hits the bottom of the stairs and back into the kitchen. I hear the scrape of the stool when she hauls herself back up.

In all the excitement and anticipation of this deployment announcement, I had forgotten just for a moment how much I must leave behind.

I sit down heavy on the edge of our unmade bed, displacing a pile of clean laundry that sends several socks falling to the floor. I have a month to get my company out the door to war. A month before I will oversee a group of men who will put their lives on the line under my command. I'm responsible for them, and this war has started to heat up. We've suffered casualties, and there's a chance not all who I bring will come home.

"Dinner!" Megan calls from downstairs, the cry of Vince at what I'm guessing is his anger over the loss of the TV show following quickly behind. I plod down the stairs and stop for a minute halfway, watching them.

Megan has this. Both kids at the table, she dishes some pasta into a couple plastic bowls that she puts down in front of the kids before filling both our plates and sprinkling cheese on top. There's a glass of water and a beer at my spot already waiting for me. She absently kisses each kid's forehead before putting the bowl of food in front of them.

The sweat of the day had matted some of her hair to her forehead, her clean face shines underneath, her gorgeous natural full lips are pinked a little from her constant worrying them with her teeth. She's in an old pair of jeans and t-shirt that is stretched over her chest. Each step she takes emphasizes that she doesn't have a bra on. I love her like this, those soft hips she hates calling to me like a beacon, urging me to grab them and lose myself in her curves.

She finally has our plates on the table and she sits at her spot, gently admonishing Victoria for finishing her milk before she's even started her noodles. Sitting here watching as she has this all so effortlessly under control, it becomes more and more clear that I'm a lucky man. I never have to worry, never wonder if my family will be okay or if Meg will be here when I get home. She's always got this.

It makes my job that much easier, knowing I never have to worry about anything back at home, not when the mortgage comes due, or when the kids need to see the dentist. Not groceries or car seat laws. She's the strongest woman I've ever met, completely able to handle this life I've thrown her into.

My greatest fear has always been that one day she'll decide it's not worth it. So instead, I try to never let her see more than she needs to, never let her know too much that might send her running. If she doesn't know what's coming, she can't leave me for it, right?

It makes sense in my head if I don't think about it too hard.

"Planning to join us, Mark?"

I realize I've been staring while they're all waiting to eat. I shake my head.

"Sorry, guys." Sitting down opposite Megan, she doesn't look at me the entire meal. Victoria sings to me in French and Vince babbles about some TV show while they both pick at the food in front of them. I try to soak in every moment. Every high-pitched giggle from Tori and happy squeal from Vince. The smell of the food, the way Megan brushes that one piece of hair back from her face every time she leans her head forward to take a bite.

When the kids and I finish with clearing the dishes, I lean down to the two of them. "Who wants to go to the store and get some squishies?"

The screeches that come in response are deafening and I stand back up, rubbing my ears. Megan has a scowl on her face probably because I never bothered asking her about it first, but I decide we won't fight tonight.

Instead, I take the towel from her hands, place it on the counter, and toss her over my shoulder. She smacks my back but soon she's laughing as I attempt to slip shoes on her flailing feet. The kids jump around us as we head out the door.

I put Megan down on the sidewalk, smoothing her hair down and kissing her lightly on the lips before we keep walking to the Macs store on the corner. By the time we get there, Vince is hanging like a monkey on my back and Tori is singing at the top of her lungs while she skips in front of us. We help them make multicoloured squishies they can never finish, and as I head to the till, I see Megan filling a little plastic bag with penny candies.

When she meets me at the till, she gives me a hip bump and looks up at me with the smile I still feel to my toes every time I see it.

"We've got this."

. . .

ONCE THE KIDS are tucked in bed, I meet Megan at the kitchen table where she's sitting with a notebook and a glass of wine. I grab a beer from the fridge and we talk over all the things that need to be done before I go. Ideas for my home leave. She's all business, and this isn't her first rodeo. Once we're done, she's more than halfway done with her bottle of red and I can tell she's exhausted just thinking of it all.

This time, when I pick her up, it's gentle, scooping my arms under her knees and pressing her head to my chest. She snuggles in, I hear her take a deep breath with her face buried against me.

I bump the door of the bedroom shut behind me and in my next step, I trip over the uniform I left on the floor earlier. I barely keep on my feet, tossing Megan onto the bed with a thud so she doesn't come down with me. She looks up at me, eyes hooded from drink and desire, giggling.

"Smooth, babe."

I just smirk, unceremoniously peeling my t-shirt and jeans off before crawling up over her.

"You know it."

Brushing the hair out of the way, I kiss gently at her neck, softly biting right behind her ear. Her giggles fade out to a quiet moan, the most beautiful sound I know. My hands just start up her t-shirt when we hear the telltale click of a door down the hall being opened before a soft knock at ours.

"Mommy? I heard noises..." Victoria's sleepy voice calls out from the other side.

I look at Megan and she laughs.

"Maybe next time."

She wiggles out from under me and it only makes it worse. I roll over, flopping on my back with a tortured moan, only making Megan laugh more as she opens the door and scoops up our daughter.

The sounds of their whispers down the hall as Megan tucks her back in lull me to sleep with a smile on my face.

*　*　*

THE WEEKS PASS IN A BLUR, and it feels like no time at all before I send off my bags, getting ready to head out. Several members of the company are meeting at a pub for a goodbye drink with others from battalion the night before we leave and my second in command has invited me. I know they won't want their boss around too long, but I decide to pop in for a moment, maybe buy a round of drinks.

When I pull up, I recognize a young corporal walking out the doors, a pretty Asian woman on his arm. Jameson, that's his name. I wish I'd had the chance to be here longer, to know my soldiers better before we leave. I tip my head to him and he gives a slight wave before ushering what must be his wife or girlfriend into a truck nearby. The quiet of that scene is a stark contrast to the rowdy bar that hits me as soon as I open the doors.

It's easy to find the table of soldiers, their voices loud and carrying across the room. There's drinks and pitchers piled on the table, different groups sitting or standing, telling stories punctuated by boisterous laughter. In the corner, I see Master Corporal Sampson, who has a cute redheaded waitress pinned by his hip against the wall as he whispers in her ear and she giggles.

I grin. It all looks exactly as it should.

"Rob! Let the poor girl get back to work!"

He turns, and the girl takes the opportunity to sneak under his arm and smooth her apron before she hurries back towards the kitchen. Her sultry smile when she looks back makes more than clear that she had hardly been a captive audience.

"Sir! Glad you came." One of my platoon commanders, Matt

Christianson saunters over, his eyes glossed with drink.

"Not staying long, Matt. Just figured I'd buy a round, say a few goodbyes." He's quick to turn back to the table of men in front of us.

"Hey, listen up, ya rowdies! Next round is on Major Lawson!"

There's hooting and hollering, and I make my way to the bar to make good on my promise. The bartender, his back to me, his solid, dark-coloured tattoos running up under his shirt sleeve, looks familiar somehow. When he turns around, I realize why.

"Jer!" He looks at me startled for a minute before grabbing my hand.

"Mark! Long time no see!"

Time has been good to Jeremy. I haven't seen him in years, since we were in Kosovo together what seems like forever ago.

"So, this is where you've been hanging out, hey?"

"A few years, ya. Got tired of lazin' around, ya know? This way I am around alcohol all day. I'm the boss so no one pisses me off and I can sleep in. Seemed like the perfect way to relax." He smiles, and we clink glasses. It's good to see him happy.

"Good to hear it, Jer."

"Laws, you leading these guys? Here for the same see-ya-later?"

I study him for a minute. I see a little envy in his eyes, as I'd expect. It never goes away.

"It is. They gave me a company! What the fuck are they thinking, right?" I lighten the mood and laugh. Jeremy and I haven't seen each other since I was a barely together lieutenant. Even as a young'n, he was always taking care of us, in the field or after a long night at the bar. Sometimes I could have sworn the man could read my mind.

He laughs with me, but takes a serious turn a little too quick.

"You're the right man for the job, Laws. Bring 'em all home."

We share a look and another clink of the glass before I feel the presence come up behind me. I'm one second too short to turn around before I feel the hand way, way too close to my ass.

"Laws!" The drunken slur behind me is all too familiar, and I turn to see Dennis over my shoulder, his oversize hand clinging a bottle of Corona, the lime floating in the middle like a dinghy on the lake. His eyes are glassed over, his weight held up heavily by the arm on the back of the chair behind me.

"Dennis. What's up, man?"

Only I know what's up. He's gone to shit. The lines on his face and bloodshot eyes aren't just from tonight. He's been barely treading water these past few years and I've been trying my best to be there, but sometimes I just don't know what to say. My career continued and he's barely holding on to his position, let alone looking to make it to the next.

We were both there. Somehow, he broke, and I wish I could figure out why the fuck it happened to him and not to me.

"All good, Laws. All good. So… when do ya take off?" His eyes avoid mine at the questions. I know he wants to come with us. He's been trying to get back there for years. He's not okay, though, and this last time when he got back from the school to battalion, the social worker wouldn't clear him to leave. They say it's so he can get healthy, but I don't know. He looks worse.

"Tomorrow morning, man. It's all a little surreal, but I'll miss having you beside me. I'll see you when I get back, hey?"

He gives me a half smile and smacks me on the back. We used to be a unit, him and I. We did everything together, from the four years in military college, to Kosovo and Afghanistan. Somewhere, though, we came to a weird impasse. I'd give up anything for my brother, but I don't know that it will ever be what he needs, anymore.

"Ya, Laws, keep your head down, hey? I'll see ya when you get back."

He saunters off and I'm quick to give a few side hugs and back slaps on my way back out. I'd rather spend these last moments at home with my family, than here with these guys. I guess I've finally grown up a bit.

When I get home, I crawl in next to Megan. Her quick breaths and stiff body next to me tells me she hasn't found her rest tonight. I doubt either of us really will. No matter how many times we do this, I don't know that this one moment gets any easier.

I pull her up close, intending to tuck her in beside me but she turns quickly, her front pressing against mine as her breath finds my neck and up to my lips. Her mouth swallows my moans as she grinds her hips into mine, the softness of her body a welcome escape. I press against her just enough to push her onto her back, my lips never leaving hers. My hand fixed under her breast tests the weight in my hand before running it up and over.

I catalogue every move. Every curve, every moan, every soft inch of flesh. She's all I need, and I need her more with every day I've known her. We can do this time apart, just like we have every time before. But my need for her, it never changes.

With a growl, I press myself into her willing body, my mind emptying of everything but the feel of her around me. While most nights we're playful, rolling around with usually at least one giggle. Tonight, we're quiet. Pleading. Imprinting on each other.

It's been seven years, but I never tire of the need to mark her as my own.

Soon she lifts her hips to mine, the soft cries from her lips only fuel my need. The very moment I feel her body respond to me, squeezing tight and holding on, is the moment I let myself go, pressing into her as though I can somehow connect her to me forever.

If only that was all it took.

No matter how hard I try to fuse her to me, by this time tomorrow, I'll be a world away.

23

MEGAN

WINTER 2006

I had mostly gotten used to the middle of the night phone calls. With the time change, it was usually around two a.m. here when Mark could call, which wasn't all that often but enough that I had grown to like the sound. Instead of the cold terror I had felt the first few times it rang.

Mark has been gone almost three months. His mid-deployment leave was weeks and weeks ago; he took the first and crappiest one so the men could have better options.

I love and loathe his leadership some days.

Really, there are some days it seemed like forever since I've seen him and other days, I barely had time to think as the time passes. With Vince in preschool a few days a week now, I'd even started a part-time job back at the same insurance broker I left after I had him. Erika had insisted she'd take me back any time, and it turned out she meant it. Working only a few days a week meant I only had him in daycare those afternoons, and saved my sanity at the same time.

When the phone rings this time, I am already awake, a growing fear in the pit of my stomach I couldn't quite place the cause of, keeping me from drifting back to sleep. I was just about to give up and turn on the light with a book when I hear the ring.

It's funny, that shrill electronic ringing is incapable of conveying anything other than noise. I could swear that time just sounded ominous. Different from all the other times.

When I answer, I can hear the crackle of the line right away, and I wait, begging silently that it will be his voice that answers. The absolute relief that floods me when it is takes me back.

"Megan." His voice is hoarse, broken.

"Are you hurt?" I've heard sometimes soldiers are given a satellite call home when they've been wounded, to talk to their spouse before news hits the media, and the fear is back.

"I'm fine. I... I lost someone."

I want to respond right away but my voice is caught in my throat. When it returns, I can't think of any words.

"Oh, Mark."

"I should have watched more closely. Checked the route better..." The static on the line makes his next words garbled and I strain my ear to the phone as if I press it closer, I can hear him through the interference.

"Corporal... twenty-nine... Someone will call... funeral..."

"Mark, I can't understand what you're saying. I'm sorry."

"It's okay. I can't talk long. I'm okay. Just remember I'm okay and I love you."

When the line goes dead before I can respond, it takes me minutes to press the off button. I sit there, on the edge of my bed, for what seems like hours. Frozen in my fear, listening to the sound of my heart pounding in my chest. Eventually I move, walking almost like a zombie down the stairs to put on some coffee.

About an hour later, just as it barely qualifies as morning instead of night, the phone rings again.

That next call is from the CO. He has the information of the widow.

He tells me they left her with a friend just a couple hours ago, that she has no children and no family nearby. I make note of her address and phone number, and he asks if I can stop in to see him on the way to visit her, so he can let me know how all of this will work for her. I try to use my most professional voice, making notes.

I look at the clock just before hanging up, realizing I don't have too long before the kids are up. My head drifts to how I'll get Tori to school, whether I can drop Vince with Cheryl at the same time.

"Megan?" his voice cuts into my fog.

"Sorry, I was just figuring out…"

"Megan, are *you* going to be okay?"

I take a moment to swallow, his unexpected kindness catching me off guard. I feel the sting in my nose that always precedes my tears.

Mark is okay. I don't get to cry, not when he's okay. Not yet.

"Yes, sir. I've got this."

AFTER A FLURRY OF ACTIVITY, getting Tori off for school, I drop Vince off to Cheryl. I don't even meet her eyes when I run out the door. She hugs me anyways, but I can't linger. I need all the focus I can find; the tears in her eyes are far too likely to bring on my own if I let them. Instead, I rush back out the door and make a quick stop for a tub of coffee and snacks at Tim Horton's before pulling up at the cute little house. The front door is already open, and I can see inside the flurry of uniforms already there. I look back at my notes. Elizabeth Amari is twenty-eight years old and lives at this home with her common-law husband, Corporal Silas Jameson. They've been together almost a decade, about the same as Mark and me. They don't have any kids.

I look back at the door. My mind wanders to what this would all look like if it was my door the notification team had knocked on instead of hers, but now is not the time to think about that. Instead, I grab my purse and the Tim's bags, and steel myself as I walk to the front door, barely knocking before someone greets me.

She's young, with blonde hair and fair skin. Tattoos twist up her arms, disappearing under the sleeves of her shirt. There are deep bags under her brown eyes.

"Elizabeth?" I ask, holding out my free hand.

"No, I'm her friend, Juliette. Beth is inside. Here, let me grab that."

I shake her hand quickly as she grabs the bags in my arms and gestures for me to come inside.

"Captain Symington just got back. He was here last night, too. He's in the living room with Beth and the Padre... I forget his name though." She sets everything down on the table and arranges cups and the snacks from the bag on the tray that is already prepared there.

"Thorne," I say absently, watching her as she makes sense of it all there. She seems to be running on autopilot.

"Yes. That's it. Padre Thorne. Are you... I mean... how are you..."

"I'm sorry, I should have mentioned. My husband, Mark, is serving with Cpl. Jameson in Afghanistan right now. I'm here to do whatever I can to make things easier. I'll start this morning coordinating some meals, but I want to be sure we know what Elizabeth's needs are before we bombard her with things."

Juliette looks at me for a moment appraisingly. I'm not offended, I'm happy it seems Elizabeth has such a great friend. Eventually she nods.

"I don't know that Beth knows what she needs right now. If people want to bring small meals, I can freeze, since it's just her, I can take care of them here. I think she's about done with the paperwork out there, so why don't we head in and you can meet her yourself."

"Thank you, Juliette."

We walk into the room and I'm first met by two men in uniform who stand to greet me. I've met them before briefly, but they give me their names and shake my hand before sitting back down. Curled up on the chair in the far end of the room is a slight woman with long, thick, black hair piled on top of her head and falling into her face. Her skin is a light brown, her features hinting at an Asian lineage. Her eyes are bloodshot and rimmed red. She goes to stand.

"No, please don't stand. My name is Megan. My husband is also in Afghanistan with Charlie Company. His name is Mark Lawson." I shake her hand and sit on the couch close to her. "I'm so sorry for your loss, Elizabeth."

She looks at me a long while.

"Thank you." Her voice cracks a little when she answers, her lips automatically pulling into a sad smile.

"I know that these officers have everything under control for you, but I want you to know I'm here and will help any way I can. I've been speaking with Col. Sars. He is the commanding officer of the battalion. Have you met him?"

She looks up at me with weary eyes and furrows her eyebrows.

"He came... I think he was here at the beginning, when they told me... I don't really remember much of that part..."

"That's okay, it's not important. No one is expecting you to remember anything right now. I just wanted you to know he knows there will be a lot of attention on you in the next little while. Captain Symington here, he will deal with all the media for you. There's also going to be a lot of offers of support and visits. The other families from the unit will want to pay respects. They'll have offers of meals and they'll want to know what they can do to help." I pause for a moment and I hear Elizabeth open her mouth and start to speak. I try to gently interrupt. "It will be my job to make sure none of that overwhelms you. All the families reaching out will be put in touch with me first. You let me know, or have your friend here let me know, if and when you're interested in visitors. I'll be sure to pass on things like meals, cards, etc. when the time is right. Would that be okay?"

Col. Sars and I had gone over all this, but I really didn't want to overstep. It felt like that's exactly what I was doing. I was relieved when she gave an almost real smile and nodded to me.

"I would appreciate that, thank you." She looks so tired. I quickly glance around the home. It's modestly decorated, overstuffed couches in front of a big TV in the corner. There's a shelf on the wall with a couple photos, looks like a vacation. An athletic, good-looking, shirtless guy with messy blonde hair has a smiling Elizabeth on his shoulders on the beach. His eyes dance, even in the photo. I drag my eyes away before the tears come.

"I will leave my number with your friend. Please don't hesitate to use it anytime in this process. Anything I can do to take some of the stress from you, I will."

She smiles shyly, and I get up, shaking hands with the officers before heading back to the kitchen where Juliette is doing dishes. She turns when she hears me come back in and smiles warmly, though her eyes aren't quite there yet.

"Your friend is lucky to have someone like you. Is there anything I can help with?"

"I'm just treading water here. I didn't know Silas well, but him and Tavish were there for me when I really needed them recently. He was really something. Beth was the only friend I had when I moved to this city, so anything I can do to help her I will."

I don't know who Tavish is, but I don't see a ring on her finger. Maybe it's her boyfriend? Either way, I'm amazed at this girl. She's clearly given more than she has just to ensure her friend has what she needs right now. I give her my number and promise to be back in a few days. I even step in and offer her a quick hug when I leave. We both seem a little awkward at it, but she softens after a second. I try to pass some strength on to her. I wish I had more to offer.

I stare at my car as I walk down the steps. When I hear the door softly click behind me, I almost falter, but I just keep staring ahead. One foot in front of the other.

I just left a widow's home. She's so young, and all I can see in my head are the dancing eyes and shock of blonde hair, the smiling face of the man in the photo on her shelf. That young man, he had someone at home waiting.

Someone just like me.

I slide behind the wheel and it's not until I press the key into the ignition that the tears come and this time, I don't wipe them away until I pull onto Cheryl's street.

24

MARK

SPRING 2007

There's a chill in the air that you know to expect when you land, but you are never quite prepared. After months and months in a place where it feels like the sun is trying to kill you as much as the enemy is, early spring on the Canadian prairies has a bite to it.

We're slow to get up out of our chairs when the bus pulls up.

Maybe slow isn't the right word, but not as fast as I think seven months ago we thought we would be. There's a sombre spirit among us, a missing breath inside the fogged windows. A joke not being told, a silence in the laughter.

I'm first out, followed by my sergeant major Bill, are we are both standing by the door, shaking the hands of our soldiers as they each head off to find their families. Some don't have anyone waiting for them. There's one I know of who got his Dear John message while we were on our way back. There's a few of his friends waiting just inside for him instead. I'll have to keep an eye on him this week.

Cpl. Cleary is the last one off. As far as I know, he's not meeting anyone here, either. I thought he had a girl, but the guys tell me he hasn't talked to her and wouldn't call his parents or grandparents, either. The look in his eyes since he got back from… well, since he got back… scares me more than most things on this deployment did.

I shake his hand, but he barely looks up. Sgt Major let his hair grow too long, but I guess it was more about picking our battles. A few stray black hairs fall into his face and he offers a fake smile briefly before turning. Instead of letting go, I grip his hand tighter and pull him in until his ear is close enough that I can speak quietly to only him in this crowded space.

"You're not alone, Cleary."

He stills a moment, then steps back, giving me a smile that stays so far from his eyes, I'm surprised he can paint it on his mouth at all. when he walks away I catch Bills eye and silently he assures me he'll keep an eye on him. I'm about to say something, anything, when a fifty-pound projectile takes me out at the legs.

"DADDY!"

A far cry from the shy reluctance she'd been at my last homecoming, Victoria is all arms and curls and tearful giggles, attaching herself to my legs so tight I struggle to pick her up. My eyes immediately dart up to catch Megan's.

With a squirming Vince on her hip pulling up the loose pink skirt she has on, her hair framing her flushed face and her eyes shining, I just stare.

She gets more damn beautiful every time I see her.

It takes me two strides to have her body crushed to me, the kids shoved to the sides in both our arms. I bury my face in her hair and breathe her in. The reaction is almost instant, and I hear her soft giggle in my ear when I'm sure she feels, even through the fabric of my combat pants, how quickly she's got me going. I'm not ashamed, I've been far too long without my wife.

Placing Tori gently on the ground next to me where she grabs hold to a leg, I use my freed hands to brush into Megan's hair and just stare at the happy tears forming in her eyes before I capture her smile with mine.

There is absolutely no kiss in the world that compares to the one that you give after coming home from war.

I must break free from her eventually, only because there's two other people I want to see, and a home and bed I desperately want to find myself in.

"Daddy!" Tori still hangs on to my leg, and now Vince tries to shove an arm between Meg and me to get in on the action. I scoop him up from her as I step back, and he holds onto my neck like his life depends on it.

"Missed you, Daddy." The burn behind my eyes threatens to overtake me at the sound of my son's wobbling voice. I close my eyes and take a deep breath before I lift my head and look at his still babyish face.

"I missed you so much, little guy. Thank you for being the man of the house while I was gone."

With that, he nods seriously and wiggles his bum to get down. I smile at that, even as exciting as seeing me is, a three-and-a-half-year-old boy stays still for no one. I place him on the ground where he runs over to the colouring table set up in a corner. I look back to Megan and grab her hips again, planting my face back in her neck.

"I want to be home," I whisper, and she lifts her hands, cupping the back of my neck.

"I want you home."

We stay that way for as long as we can, even as I hear my men disperse around me. The cry of babies and the squeal of toddlers, the odd sniffle from a wife or a mom. Even the eyes of the jaded military teenagers aren't dry. It's been a long deployment.

I feel Megan stiffen and I follow her gaze to Cpl. Cleary. He's being handed something by the duty officer onsite.

"I didn't know if I'd find him, so I asked Lt. Froese if he would make sure his keys got to him. His friend Juliette dropped his truck off."

I watch as Tavish takes the keys with a shrug, looking around the room for an invisible presence.

"Why didn't she come herself?"

"I'm not sure. I don't think she felt like she was wanted here."

Tavish looks at the keys for a long moment before he shoulders his ruck and grabs his barrack box and heads to the door. I'm a few steps behind him, out in the parking lot and about to go to him when Megan grips my arm. My gaze lingers, but I see Bill ambling towards him so I turn my attention away.

"Mark, that's Beth Jameson."

By now, Vince is back, and I haul him up on my shoulders and Tori on my hip, following Megan's gaze to two young women sitting in a beat-up old car at the far end of the lot. I recognize Beth right away from the photos. Her striking long, black hair hangs loose behind her. As she gets out of the passenger seat, it blows in the crisp spring breeze. The tiny blonde girl slowly standing from the driver's side watches her protectively as I approach. It's almost comical, the fierceness in the eyes of such a tiny little thing. Up close, I can see she means business and I respect her loyalty.

I place Vince and Tori down and they stick there with their mom as I continue my walk towards Cpl. Jameson's widow. I know they weren't really married, but it means the same thing. I failed this woman, and even though my legs bring me a step closer every moment, my heart is seized deeper in my chest with every breath.

She's stopped where she is, right in front of me, her dark

eyes shining and rimmed red. She doesn't look defeated, though, more filled with a reluctant acceptance. I stand there for too long, trying to find words, before she steps entirely forward and wraps her arms around my neck.

I feel my bags hit the ground as I reach up and tentatively hold on. I wonder if she realizes she's holding me up as I attempt to say something, anything.

All that comes out of my mouth is, "I'm sorry." Over and over in her ear, I barely even feel the tears on my face as I repeat it like it's a prayer. A prayer for forgiveness. Because that's exactly what it is.

Beth leans her head back, leaving her arms holding on and looks me in the eye. I resist the overwhelming urge to turn away from her gaze.

"This. Is. Not. On. You." She punctuates every word and I feel like a fool, I can't even begin to hold the sob back. I swallow hard and after a moment that seems like forever, she steps back just as I hear Victoria's giggle behind me.

"Welcome home, Major... Mark. Enjoy your family." I want to see bitterness in her face but all I see is honest happiness for me in her small smile. I don't know if that makes it better or worse. I just nod, and turn back to Megan who looks like I feel, the tears falling unchecked down her flushed cheeks. I grab the kids again and head over towards the van, just concentrating on putting one foot in front of the other and trying not to let the guilt of this walk home paralyze me before I make it back.

I AM CONCERNED that Tori might not be breathing while she tells me every story of everything that's happened to her since I saw her last. The drive home is just one long sentence from her mouth, everything from the new kid at school with the pretty blonde hair and the lisp to the houses being built at the end of the street. Her teacher has a new puppy. Her cousins got a fish named Bob, but he died. Again. By the time we pull into the driveway, my head is spinning to the sound of the most gorgeous high-pitched giggle ever heard.

We give the kids more time than we should once we're home before sending them to bed, even though it's close to midnight. Meg pops some popcorn while I look at the changes to their bedrooms, the drawings they've made, the new boots they just got. Vince has ten thousand new stuffies at least, and they all have names, so it takes a while. By the time I have him in bed and lie down to read Tori a book, it feels like I've been awake for weeks. Suddenly, Megan's hand is on my shoulder and I open my eyes, my head laying half on top of *Where the Wild Things Are*, with Tori's tiny snores right in my ear.

I roll off the teeny twin bed and gently to the floor before getting up, so I don't wake her. Megan grabs the book from the pillow and puts it back on the shelf and we both make our way back to the hall, clicking the door quietly behind us. All the exhaustion I felt only seconds before vanishes when I catch a look at Megan in the light from the open bathroom door. Her face is clean from makeup, just how I like it, and she's thrown on a nightgown. Long and transparent green with a deep slit up one side all the way to her waist and thin straps barely holding up her breasts. She's radiant. It takes me so long to drink her in, the curves of her hips and chest, her light hair framing her gorgeous face. She's everything.

"Fuck, babe, I've got maybe three minutes in here. I feel like you've wasted this absolutely stunning look on tonight, I'm already ready to burst." I have my mouth over hers in a matter of a second, and we fumble our way to the door. I can feel the heat from her even through the sweatpants I'd thrown on. My hands are everywhere at once and I want nothing more than to have all of her. Now.

My self-control after all this time is worn to barely anything. My mind loves how blank she makes it. All I can think about is the beauty in front of me and the need for her to be underneath. Backing her into our bedroom, I press her down onto the bed so I can devour her, thankful that it takes no time at all to feel her tremble under me. I'm right there with her the moment I sink into her heat, and while I'm not ashamed of how quickly we're left panting next to each other on the bed, it's not my finest moment either. But that's what all that time apart can do to you.

I'm starting to drift off on this soft bed next to the woman I love, content for the first time in months, when the phone's shrill ring has me jumping ten feet up. Megan answers, it takes me far longer to get my bearings.

"Mark? It's for you."

I look at the receiver a moment before I put it to my ear.

"Ya?"

"Hey, Mark." I hear the CO's voice in my head and I stiffen.

"Sir?"

"I'm sorry, I hate to do this. It's Dennis Peters. I'm sorry, Mark. He took his own life tonight. I'm going to need you to come in."

And just like that, it's like I'll never truly rest.

25

MEGAN

SPRING 2007

He presses the off button on the receiver and just stares at it for a moment.

"Mark?" I put my hand on his bicep, but he doesn't even notice. He's completely lost in whatever that call told him. There's a cold feeling up my spine, settling in my stomach. He's shaken, bad, and I can't imagine what could affect him this way.

He still doesn't look at me when he finds his voice. "It's Dennis."

"On the phone?" It didn't sound like Dennis; the voice was only vaguely familiar.

"No, that was the CO. He… it's Dennis. He's gone."

"Gone? What do you mean, gone?"

"He killed himself tonight."

The air between us is thick while I try to process what he just said. I picture Dennis in our kitchen, pretending to steal snacks from the kids while he waits to drive Mark to a mess dinner. He was smiling, laughing. He can't have done this.

Suddenly, Mark is up, searching in drawers before pulling on an old pair of jeans and t-shirt. "I have to go in..."

No! No, no, no, no, no... I'm filled with guilt at my immediate response. This was my night. Our night. All the plans I had for our night, our day, our homecoming fizzle before my eyes and my first response is anger. I swallow it, hard in my throat.

"Do you need me to..."

"No. Go back to sleep."

He's out the bedroom before I even open my mouth to respond, and then I hear the garage door slam. It opens again a moment later and I hear him rustling around. He forgot the keys. I start getting out of bed. He's really in no state to drive, and he hasn't been driving for almost seven months. This shouldn't be how he jumps back in. But the door is shut again before I even get pants on, and this time, I hear the garage door open and the truck start.

I make my way to the kitchen and grab a glass of water. I sit down on the living room couch and flick on the TV. I couldn't even tell you what show is on. All I can think of is Dennis, and I stare at the chair in the kitchen where he sat last with us for dinner. We only saw him a time or two after we moved here before Mark left. When we lived in St. Jeans, he would come down for the weekend, sleep on the couch, and bum around with Mark. Sometimes we wouldn't see him for weeks, but he was always around somewhere. Always popping up.

I guess not anymore.

I hate this, not knowing what happened, what's going on, what it means. I find myself absently rubbing the spot on my chest, the one close to my armpit.

The spot with the little, dangerous bump.

I found it a few weeks ago in the shower, a little lump that hadn't been there before. I tried to brush it off, but I finally caved and went in to see my doctor. He sent me right away for a mammogram, which showed that little tiny flaw that is so ominous. I have a biopsy this morning. A tiny little syringe will test my fate.

I was going to talk to Mark about it in the morning. When I first found the lump, I cried for almost an hour in the bath. All I could see was my mother wasting away as I fingered the little bump that wasn't there before. I could have told Mark, but by the time he was able to call, on the crackling phone line with only a few minutes to spare, I couldn't get the words out. There was nothing he could do from there, and it ended up being Cheryl and Erika that came and drank wine with me and held my hand and took me to the first appointment. There was no sense bothering him when he couldn't help anyways.

Then I didn't want to ruin our homecoming moments, so I decided I'd wait and tell him this week, once we were settled. Give him a chance to adjust first. But now, I don't know how he will react. Telling him seems almost cruel, with the way his head will be these next few days. Instead, I decide right then to just wait. He can't change anything now, and we don't know for sure if there's even a reason to worry. I'll go to my appointment in the morning and I won't bother him unless there's a reason to.

That makes sense, right?

All I know is that right now, I can't imagine adding anything else to the burden I can see in his eyes. Not when I watched his pain when he hugged Beth. Not when I saw his expression after that phone call. I can wait, at least until I know more.

There's a soft light filtering in from the living room window when the sound of the garage door wakes me from a sleep I didn't even know I'd fallen into. I'm still half-sitting, half-lying down on the couch when I open my eyes and see Mark open the door, toeing off his boots. I can tell he doesn't see me when I watch as he stops for a moment by the entrance to the hallway, running his hands through his hair and letting out a deep breath. It occurs to me he is steeling himself to see me, trying to put himself together before I have the chance to see him. It makes me irrationally hurt that he feels like he hides himself from me, even a little.

I close my eyes and make a soft noise as though I'm just waking up, and when I open my eyes this time, Mark looks right at me.

"What are you doing over there?"

"I must have fallen asleep waiting for you." I give him my kindest smile, but his face doesn't change. It just looks broken down, and he makes his way over and falls onto the couch next to me.

"Mark… what happened?"

"I just… I guess someone found him in his apartment. He hung himself. There's no note or anything, so I just… Fuck. I don't know. I mean, I knew, but I didn't *know*."

I put my hand over his and he looks over at me sadly. I don't know what to say, so I just tug a little. He eventually almost falls over, his head landing on my lap where I softly brush his hair in my hands and he closes his eyes.

"I'm so tired, Meg."

It's no time at all before his soft snores are the only sound in the room.

I can hold him like this, but I have no idea what to do with him when he wakes up.

"Daddy! You're still here!" I open my eyes to two little people, crawling onto Mark and me on the couch. I try to move but my entire body hurts. I wasn't made to sleep in a ball on an old couch and from the noises Mark makes next to me, neither was he, no matter how many worse places he's slept.

Both kids chatter away while I try to bring back the memories of how I ended up here from that content place I had found last night in our post-sex bliss on the bed.

Dennis.

Mark is just blinking awake. I watch his face go through the motions of rehashing last night and then tucking it away and grabbing the kids in bear hugs, tickling and generally causing chaos as they screech happily. Twelve hours and it could almost be easy to forget he just got home from war, this next crisis refusing to let the focus stick on us.

He must go into work this morning, so I start on some breakfast while he attempts to walk to our bedroom with a giggling child on each leg. I hear them squeal as he dumps them on the bed, and they come running back out to the kitchen to leave him to get dressed. I throw pancakes in front of them and frown. Mark still isn't out.

Heading up to our room, I gently nudge the door open. He's sitting on the bed in his boxers, his head in his hands. I watch silently, the gentle rise and fall of his shoulders, his hands folded on the back of his neck. He didn't hear me enter and I have the first opportunity to really look at him in the light. He's smaller than usual, the cords of muscles that usually follow his big shoulders to his biceps have thinned and the tiny bit of softness he generally carries above his hips is gone completely. He's nothing but lean muscle now, and I can't help but notice the slightly raised marks on his biceps from that IED. I know he hates them, they serve to him only a reminder of the failure he thinks he was when Cpl. Jameson didn't make it and he did, instead of what they truly are. A reminder of the kind of leader that reacted quickly and ensured the safety of all the other men under his command, even in the chaos and despite his own injuries.

His breathing is steady, but ragged. The tension in his hands at the nape of his neck is evident by his whitening knuckles. I hear him let out a soft shudder and I reach forward, touching him softly on the top of his head.

He jumps without warning, his forehead making contact

with my chin on the way up, and I land unceremoniously on my ass in front of him.

"Shit. Shit, Megan, are you okay?" He's breathing heavily like he just ran up the stairs. I rub my chin. Nothing hurts but my pride.

"I'm fine, Mark." I get up and look at him. His eyes are red and swollen, and it occurs to me that he was up here crying. It breaks my heart he wouldn't share that moment with me, let me comfort him. He hasn't shared anything with me at all since he's been home. If I'm honest, he hasn't ever shared that kind of pain with me, and I know he carries more than just this deployment.

"I just came to tell you breakfast is on the table. I didn't mean to scare you."

"You didn't scare me. I was just startled, that's all. Are you sure you're okay?"

"I'm fine." I keep watching him until he finally says something.

"I'm good. I just... I'm good, Megan." He gives me a pained, fake smile, but I don't call him on it since Victoria yells something from downstairs about spilled syrup and I head with a sigh in her direction, taking one last look at his broken eyes before I go.

The kids head out for school and I leave for work around the same time I see Mark emerge from upstairs with his uniform on, ready to head in. A quick kiss lingers just a moment before we both head in different directions.

I have my appointment today, but I'll be done before he even gets back from work. We can talk after, when there's more time.

That's what I tell myself going out the door, but I wonder if there will ever be time.

* * *

TRUE TO MY HEART, I just never do find the time, even as days just keep moving, even when I feel like I just need a moment for it to stop so I can breathe. The days blend together again as the week continues. Mark starts his vacation time, but he still leaves early in the morning, usually even before the kids and me, to head to the gym. We've talked, we've even gone on a date while my sister babysat, but he won't tell me anything. The only time he smiles is with the kids and even then, sometimes I wonder if he's going out of his way to avoid them. I know he needs time coming back but I wonder if he needs more than just time this go around. How am I supposed to tell the difference?

We haven't even come close to getting used to him here at home and next week, he has to head to Dennis' hometown, the booming metropolis of Flin Flon Manitoba. He's supposed to lead the team that will be part of the military ceremony for Dennis' funeral. I tried suggesting, only once, that maybe he wasn't in the right place to do it, but there is no stopping him. I can't really blame him, even if I want to protect him from the hurt. I hope this will offer him some closure, some relief from the guilt, but I'm worried it will be the opposite. Dennis' parents blame the military for his suicide and their anger seems to extend to Mark. To anyone, really. I can't blame them, much, I suppose. I can't imagine what that kind of pain would cause a person to do. But the fact that anyone would try to put more on his shoulders right now pisses me off.

My biopsy results will come in while he's gone. I still haven't told him. Is there supposed to be a good time to tell my husband, who just got back from war and just lost his best friend, that you are waiting to see if you have cancer?

If there is, I don't know it.

By Friday, I swing in the door from work, exhausted. I've been trying to ignore the bags under my eyes, and write off the bagginess in my pants as stress and excitement over Mark coming home, but I know, deep down, I'm fooling myself. I'm so tired, all the time. It's not for lack of sleep. Most nights, I flop into bed around ten and read until I fall asleep. I have no idea when Mark crawls in next to me. He's almost always downstairs in front of the TV, or outside in the garage, or out at the pub with 'friends.'

He's not fooling me; his friends are home with their wives.

He's drinking alone.

At least, I hope he is, considering the alternative I try not to think about.

The house is eerily quiet when I step inside. I don't hear a peep from the kids. With Mark home on leave, he's been picking them up after school, so I don't have to rush or send them to Cheryl's. I hear a rumble from the basement, the sound of speakers up too loud. Without even taking my shoes off, I take the stairs two at a time, finding Mark on the couch, CGI blood splattering over the TV screen as Spartan warriors fight it out on screen. This is the movie I didn't want to watch with him this weekend. He just got home from war. I can't understand why he'd want to immerse himself in more of it. The speakers are so loud with the grunts and slashes of the fight that he still hasn't heard me. His eyes are lidded while he's slouched on the couch watching. There's a couple empty bottles of Keith's on the table. It's four fifteen in the afternoon. The kids should have been picked up half an hour ago.

"MARK!" I yell from right next to him just to get his attention and he jumps. For a half second, I think he might tackle me but I see the recognition on his face quickly. Then it's panic.

"Oh, shit! Meg, what time is it?"

I'm already halfway up the stairs. "Too late, Mark." The kids must have walked to Cheryl's. That's their usual schedule, when Mark is away or working, since she lives just a block from their school.

I fume the entire way to her house. It's not far, just ten minutes, but it gives me enough time to mentally list all the ways Mark is failing at life since he's been home. He's shut down communication. He avoids the kids. He avoids ME. It's been days and he hasn't touched me since his first night home, opting instead to come to bed long after I've gone to sleep.

I know he's hurting. But so am I. I guess it's not fair, since he doesn't even know everything going on in my world. How can I tell him when he's checked out already? I just finished months and months of worry, of handling every little thing on my own, only to have him come home and everything stay as though he was still gone.

I want him to get mad. I'd rather he yell at me, or fight with me about the new dishes, anything. I think I'd rather have an angry husband than one that acts like he's not even here.

When I pull up to Cheryl's place, the front door opens and I can see Tori and Vince pulling their backpacks off their backs and kicking off their shoes. Cheryl is in the front entrance and I catch her eye as I pull up into the driveway. The last thing I need right now is her judgement over this, but there's no way around it.

"Hey, munchkins!" I say in an overly cheery voice even I don't believe, scooping Vince up and putting him on my lap as I sit on the bench at the entrance and put his shoes back on.

"Sorry! We're gonna head home now, okay?"

Victoria just stops what she's doing, one shoe on and one off, her backpack on the floor and her hair a complete mess of black curls only partially held together by an elastic on top of her head, and stares at me.

"Is Daddy gone again?" There's no emotion to her question, no concern. She asks it the same way she would ask about the weather, or if we were having spaghetti for dinner. My heart sinks.

"No, honey, Daddy was just busy with important things this afternoon, but we will see him when we get home."

Cheryl gives me a pointed look, but I ignore it, thankful there's nothing she would say in front of the kids. Unfortunately, with their shoes and jackets back on, they both run excitedly outside and into the van, bickering with each other the whole way about who gets to sit where, while I watch from the doorway and wait for Cheryl's lecture that I know is coming.

"That's bullshit, isn't it? Did he fall asleep in front of the TV? Get lost on the way home from the pub? Have you even seen him today?"

The problem with having your sister for your best friend is that she knows everything, and she holds no punches. I find myself regretting my honesty with her these last few days.

"He's at home, Cheryl; he just lost track of time. He's not used to all of this."

Cheryl's gaze doesn't leave mine.

"You haven't told him, have you?"

"What am I supposed to say? He needs time, Cheryl. He needs to get used to being home before I throw more on his plate. It could be nothing anyways."

Cheryl's look softens slightly at that.

"You're right, sweetie. It might be nothing. Just… Remember when he was home to visit?"

Mark's mid-deployment leave had been mostly a disaster. He spent most of the time hiding from all the people who wanted to visit, and almost never slept in our bed. Whenever I'd wake in the night, he would be downstairs, the soft murmur of the news channel from the TV drifting up. Right before he went back, we had been fighting over him leaving it on while the kids were there all the time. I didn't think they needed to see that much reality. He thought they might as well know it all now.

We barely made up before he got back on the plane, and only because neither of us wanted him to leave mad.

"It takes time, Cheryl. We can't imagine what it was like for him. I just need to give him time. Besides, it's not like his leave. At least then he would touch me." The words are out of my mouth before I have time to reconsider and I make a face as soon as I say them. I was hoping to avoid rehashing my wine-soaked confession from earlier in the week about how Mark hadn't even shown interest since that first night.

"Still? Do you think…"

"No! Just stop. He needs space, and we can do that. I've done this before, it's just a little harder this time. It will be okay, *we* will be okay. He just needs time."

Cheryl is quiet for a long time and I start towards the door when she grabs me in a hug.

"I sure hope so, Meg."

I swallow my voice that screams in my head, "I hope so, too."

For the first time in eight years, I honestly don't know.

26

MARK

PRESENT

It's snowed here overnight, which doesn't surprise me in the prairies anymore. I remember my first years here from the island. I couldn't believe the weather, and I wore winter jackets almost year-round. Now, however, the cold has grown on me, and like the natives, I usually only throw on a heavy sweater before I head out most cold fall days, snow or not. It looks like today, I'll be scraping some of the snow off the car that I was too exhausted to even pull into the garage last night.

Turns out, being at home with kids is hard.

It's not that I ever thought Meg had it easy, but raising these two hellions of ours is like trying to tame a tornado. Two tornados, and they're never blowing in the same fucking direction, either.

Cheryl offered to keep them. I might even have taken her up on it too if the offer hadn't been laced with the idea I couldn't look after them myself. So, my pride spoke before my brain and

I've spent the last week regretting my inability to accept help. By the time I get the kids to school, drop in at work for a half day trying to catch up on the school work they've officially transferred my staff college year to distance learning, then head back to get Vince, stick him in front of the TV and do more school work from home, then pick Tori up and head to the hospital… There's been at least two days Vince has had to remind me to feed him lunch. I have yet to tackle dinner; the hospital cafeteria has taken care of that for me, thankfully. Then it's home and getting them in bed, with I swear seventy-five books and promises of anything short of a pony to get them to sleep.

Who am I kidding? At this point, I'd buy them a damn pony.

When the house is quiet should be my moment to relax, but instead, the empty space and lonely bed only serve to remind me of why I'm here. Inevitably, that feeling sends me to a bottle of scotch and keeps me there until I can't keep my eyes open any longer and I pass out asleep on the couch.

I can't seem to face that bed alone. So that's been my days, and nights, for a week now.

It's Saturday morning and I'm up before the kids, a cup of coffee in my hands as I stare out the window at the last few fluffy flakes falling in the light of the streetlamp. We can bring Megan home today, at least that's what they've said. Her infection is under control, now that the antibiotics are finally working, and her fever is gone. If she continues to do well, she can start chemo again soon.

Chemo.

Again.

My wife was having chemo treatments and I didn't even know she had cancer.

It's been a long week of piecing together what exactly is going on for her. She was diagnosed with Stage 2 breast cancer, and had a lumpectomy before starting chemo. She apparently won't be needing radiation, since as far as they can tell, they removed all the cancer from her body and the chemo is more preventative to ensure it doesn't return, or that any scrap left behind is killed. According to her and her oncologist, a small, grey-haired man with glasses that seem too small for his face and a scowl that tells me he doesn't appreciate me showing up halfway through this process, things have been going as to plan and they weren't expecting any further complications. But until they retest after the chemo is done, and then every year after for five years, he can't give us any guarantee it's gone.

I want a fucking guarantee.

Well, very few people care what I want.

So, it turns out the only reason she's in the hospital now, fighting through an infection that could have cost her life, is because she's also working full time, raising two kids on her own, and trying her damnedest to be superwoman, leading to not enough sleep, not enough decent rest, and exposure to a bug probably brought home by one of the kids. Absolutely no amount of convincing will ever get the doctors or nurses in this place to not believe 100% this is my fault.

That's fine, no one will ever convince me of that, either.

So instead, I've thrown myself into learning everything Megan needs like it's my job. Which it should have been, right from the beginning. I don't think I've slept yet, spending my nights on the internet learning everything I can about breast cancer, about treatment options, and how to care for someone during chemo. I learn about support groups and heredity genes, special testing and even nausea candies and heated blankets for your hospital bed during treatment. I resist the urge to buy everything on the page. I don't think this is the kind of thing I can make up for with a gift, and I honestly have no idea what she already has. She hasn't lost her hair; it's thinner but the doctor said it's not too unusual it's still there because she's only a couple treatments in. I guess she was putting off shaving it. I wonder if she was going to buy wigs. How she was planning to explain to me when she was fucking bald.

When I finally got up the nerve to head to our home last week, it was surreal. Megan had never been meticulous about cleaning; she'd always insisted she was more worried about being a mom and enjoying her life than keeping a perfect house, but it had always been put together.

Instead, it looked like no one had put anything away in weeks. The fridge seemed to be filled exclusively with ginger ale, apple juice, and kid snacks. No less than six Costco cracker boxes and Lipton soup mix containers were on the floor of the pantry and the freezer held only frozen pizzas, toaster waffles, and chicken nuggets.

Walking into our bedroom, I froze. The bed was a disaster, the comforter on the floor with only the sheet in a tangled mess on top. The door to the closet open, and I could see for the first time how sad it looked with half of it almost entirely empty. A few kid's books lay on the side of the bed I'm usually on. A pile of pill containers was next to the lamp on the nightstand, along with a bottle of ginger ale and a bucket. I pictured her throwing up into it before having to drag herself up to the bathroom to clean it out, one or both kids in the bed beside her. The room still smelled faintly like vomit, which is probably why the window was open slightly even though this time of year, it makes the entire room freezing.

It looked exactly how you would expect the bedroom of someone who is sick and completely alone to look. The whole house did.

I stared at it for what seemed like forever, and then decided to clean it. And then realized I had no idea where the carpet cleaner is, or where the dusting mitts, or cleaner are. I mean, it couldn't be hard to find if I looked, but that's enough to paralyze me. I thought of calling Cheryl to ask, but the idea of giving her

FIGHT FOR HOME

even more ammo against me had me putting my phone back in my pocket. Instead, I backed right out of the room.

Since Cheryl still had the kids that week while I settled things with work and, well basically just myself, I found myself at the pub that night, staring at the bar top like it would answer my questions while Jeremy poured me a beer.

"Back here for a course, Mark?"

"Naw... I had to come back for family."

"Why, is Megan okay?"

I open my mouth to say sure, because that seems like the right answer, to just assure everyone that everything is fine. Instead, I find myself spewing the entire story to the coaster I'm peeling apart in front of me. Jeremy doesn't say a word, only nods when he should or makes short little noises to encourage me to continue. When I've got it all out, I take a long pull from my now almost warm beer.

"Shit, Mark."

I laugh but it comes out more of a snarl.

"Yup. Shit."

I'm silent a while longer and Jeremy turns around for a moment to make another drink for someone. When he's facing me again, he slides another pint of Keith's my way and then plants both hands on the bar.

"So?"

"What do you mean, so? Why would she keep this from me? That's not okay, Jer!"

He steps back a minute, contemplating I guess or whatever goes on inside that head of his. He can't help analyzing us, and it's only mildly annoying right now. I guess I was hoping for a bit of his encouragement today.

"How many birthday parties has she thrown alone? Anniversaries? How many babies she delivered without you there, how much kid puke has she cleaned up on her own? She did all that because she's a strong woman, Mark."

"Of course she is! That's not the point..."

"Oh, I dunno about that."

Jeremy goes back to tending bar for a while and I sit, stewing in my own juices a little longer until a familiar figure comes out from the kitchen.

"Mr. Lawson?" Juliette skips over to me. "You're back!" She gives me a little hug. The girl is adorable.

When I go to open my mouth to say hi, she stops me.

"Oh! You must know now..."

I just stare at her, dumbfounded.

"I mean... oh, shit."

Jeremy laughs at her.

"Relax, Jules. He knows."

"Oh, good! So, you obviously came home, how is she doing?"

"I'm confused, you know?"

"Yes... well, I mean, Jason was the one who saw Megan at the hospital when he went in for a follow up..."

I put it together.

"Right. So, he's the one who told Matt."

She just nods, looking sheepish.

"I can only imagine what you guys think of me."

"Well, you're here now, Mr. Lawson."

"Mark, Juliette."

She smiles. "Sure. Anyways, is there anything you need?"

"Actually, I was just about to ask Jer if he knew a cleaning service I could call. I don't even know how to start on our place."

Juliette looks at me a moment and shakes her head before turning around.

"Hey, Beth! You free tomorrow to give Meg's house a good cleaning before she gets out of the hospital?"

I see Cpl. Jameson's widow look up from where she is sitting over in a booth with a monster-sized man, a soldier I vaguely recognize.

"Of course, just pick me up on your way."

Juliette turns back around to me.

"Problem solved. We'll be there around nine, that work?"

I open my mouth to protest but I feel Jeremy's hand on my shoulder.

"Just say yes, Subbie," he says, using the nickname for the lowest ranking, brand new officers, which is what I had been when we met over a decade ago.

"I'm a fucking major, Warrant," I mumble under my breath, and he just laughs. Juliette is gone back to work before I can say another word.

THE HOUSE LOOKED like a show home by the time I got back from the hospital that next day. Juliette and Beth were nowhere to be found but there were flowers and chocolates on the kitchen counter, beer and groceries in the fridge, and a note on the whiteboard that said, "Thanks for letting us help!" with the girls' numbers underneath in case I needed anything else.

Damn women. They almost hit one of my feelings.

Looking around the place now, though, you can only barely tell it had ever been that clean, especially only a week ago. Once the kids came back here, between them, school, work, and the hospital, I'm a complete mess. I can't even deny it. I have no idea this is how Meg was living, adding in her appointments and treatments and illness.

How does someone manage this?

Tiny but somehow loud footsteps make their way down the stairs and I feel a soft little body crawl its way up until an eager, sleep-woozy face staring right into mine.

"Mom comes home today?"

"That's what they say, little man. How about some breakfast and we see about going to pick her up?"

"Pancakes!"

I set Vince down and go about making the only thing I really know how to, box pancakes. I just have to add water, so it's become a staple here.

It takes less time than it has been but probably still longer than Meg would need before I have them at the hospital, running into their mom's room.

"Mommy! Can you come home? For real? Can you?"

I almost smiled at the innocence behind his words until I see his mom's face. There's pain behind her smile that she'd never let him see.

"Yes, sweetie, the doctor says I can come home."

Vince bounds up onto the bed and Tori sits on the edge while Megan tells them about nurses and meals, and the fun things that happen to her at the hospital, as though it's the best vacation possible.

He is five.

I know he knows she is making it up.

She is still all in. Because that's how parenthood works.

She's banking on me not knowing that.

WHEN THE TIME COMES, the hospital insists on a wheelchair. She fights. With everything in her, to not need one. Finally, I bend down, tired of the argument, and tell her I will move her from the room to the car right now. She stills. The fight ends. And I have a moment to wheel her into the elevator, one uncomfortable moment as though the woman I have known for a decade is a stranger to me. I'm expected to watch her fend for herself while I'm standing right here.

I won't.

She is mine to care for and I will.

It's a quiet ride, punctuated only by the chatter of Vince in the backseat.

FIGHT FOR HOME

When we get home, I scoop her up in my arms and head upstairs to our room.

"Mark! What the hell!"

"Relax, Meg."

I miss when she would melt into me when I picked her up. Instead, she sits stiff in my arms, refusing to relax even a moment. Once I get to our room, I take a deep breath. At least this part of the house is still immaculate, with clean bedding and spotless floors.

"You made the bed?" Megan looks at me incredulously as I place her down gently on the comforter.

"I told you the girls came and cleaned for me."

"That was over a week ago, Mark!"

"I..." Whatever, I'm all in. "I couldn't bring myself to sleep here without you."

Megan just stares at me a moment, her face scrunched up like she's trying to figure something out.

"Sometimes it takes me awhile to get used to sleeping here *with* you," she whispers and I turn away. How can we stand together when we're coming at life from opposite places?

"I'm ah... I'm going to take Tori and Vince to the grocery store and we'll pick up pizza on the way back. Take a nap, yeah?"

Megan shrugs.

"I guess. I can make dinner, Mark."

"You can, I'm sure. But you won't. Stay in bed, Megan, I mean it."

Her face hardens and I'm sure I'm in for a fight. I just click the door behind me and head out. We have plenty of time to fight over it all later.

I hope.

27

MEGAN

SPRING 2007

I have breast cancer.
I walk out of the appointment in a daze. My brain is still trying to process the information about my surgery options, chemo, stages.

It's supposed to be a positive that it doesn't seem to be in my lymph nodes. The doctor recommends a lumpectomy, just an easy surgery that will remove the lump itself, not an entire breast. After that, preventative chemo. It doesn't look like I need radiation.

This is all a lot to take in.

None of it sounds simple, or easy, or quick, which are words the doctor kept using, like that would make me believe it.

Erika squeezes my hand next to me as we walk to the car. Cheryl has tears staining her face. This whole thing is easier for Erika; she's never seen someone waste away to cancer like Cheryl and I have. She's never seen the pain and loss and heartbreak of it all. The messy parts, the terrifying parts.

I wish I hadn't.

The doctor's told us a thousand things. How treatments have changed. How I caught this earlier than Mom did. How my chances were so much better than hers were. The thing about odds, though, is there's always that percentage, no matter how small, that make up the worst case. And for those people, odds didn't much matter, did they?

"We're going to get through this," Cheryl says at the same time.

Erika asks, "You going to finally tell Mark?"

I open the car door and we all slide in.

"Yes. We're going to make it." I try to sound a hundred percent more confident than I am. "And yes, of course, I'll tell Mark. Once he's back from Manitoba."

He left earlier this week. Our goodbye was awkward, forced almost. Neither of us was prepared for it, or wanted to acknowledge what it was about. He won't even talk about Dennis. I tried, almost every night, to mention him, to ask how Mark was feeling, to even just remember a story of Dennis. Mark just shut it down. Doesn't want to hear it. Instead, he insists he's 'going out with friends,' but I know he's still just drinking alone. The only reason I haven't said anything is I know his old friend Jeremy is a bartender there. I just hope beyond hope that at least maybe he's talking to him, since he sure as hell won't share with me.

Maybe that's not fair, since I haven't told him about any of this year. How am I supposed to do that when he doesn't let me in? He's on edge and I'm scared he'll break.

Today was the funeral in Flynn Flon Manitoba. Mark is leading the group that went to be pallbearers and honour guard. Dennis' family wanted all of it, the whole military deal for the funeral and so it will be a long and formal affair. The opposite of Dennis. I think all the ceremony, though, keeps Mark detached.

It's the point when he reattaches that scares me.

Cheryl, Erika, and I stay up late. Paul watches the kids and they fall asleep at Cheryl's well before I get him to give me a ride back to my place. I've had too much wine, but I don't want to stay there. I tell them I just really need a hot bath and my own jammies, but the truth is, I'm crying before the door is all the way closed behind me and I'm completely alone in this big, empty house.

Still in my boots, I fall onto the couch. With no one here, I don't even bother to cover my face as the tears turn to loud, gulping sobs. My nose runs into my mouth and my chest heave with every breath I manage through the hiccups.

I have no idea how I'm going to do this.

* * *

"Meg!"

I blink my eyes open and it feels like sandpaper under my lids.

Where am I?

It takes me a moment to process the boots still on my feet and the couch cushion under my face. Apparently, I never made it off the couch last night.

Great.

"MEG!"

I hear the one syllable of my name as though it's ten as it pounds into my hungover brain. I feel like I ate cotton balls for dinner. I open my mouth but can't even answer past the dryness. Getting up, I slowly pad into the kitchen and see the trail of green that heads up towards our bedroom.

Mark.

Mark must have gotten home and gone straight up to our room without seeing me there on the couch.

"I'm in the kitchen!" I call up as loudly as I can, but I swear the sound has a vibration that goes right down the back of my neck to my stomach.

I hear him thumping around up there while I grab a glass of orange juice and the bottle of painkiller from above the microwave. I'm just swallowing a handful down when he appears at the bottom of the stairs.

"Meg, I got… Wait… are you going somewhere? Why do you have your boots on? Where are the kids?"

I catch a look at my reflection in the microwave glass, my face swollen and eyes puffy, my hair plastered on one side of my face. I can still feel the indent from a cushion seam on my cheek. I'm still in yesterday's clothes, my light jacket halfway done up and my black boots still on my feet.

"Did you just get home? Where's the car? What the fuck is going on, Meg?"

I'm still staring. I don't know how to answer. Now should be when I tell him everything, but he's making me so mad, I don't want to tell him a damn thing. I think I cried out all my fight last night.

"Welcome home, hey? The kids are at Cheryl's. I had a long night. I'm going to get them now, if that' okay with you." I spit back out at him.

"Whatever. Meg. Fine. My posting message came in today,"

"What?"

I knew it was coming, the message posting us away from here again. In all of this, I completely forgot. Completely forgot that I knew we were scheduled to move across the country again. How could I forget that?"

"The posting message? It's for Toronto, like we thought. One year while I'm in school."

"I can't go," I blurt out without thinking. All I know is I'm scheduled to have surgery here in just under two months. I guess we're going to have this conversation now, once I explain.

"Fine. I figured you'd rather stay. I'll go by myself. It's no big deal."

I wasn't expecting this. I was expecting a fight, for him to want to know why, for him to be mad at the idea of splitting up our family.

Not just give up.

"What do you mean you'll go alone? What will happen to us?"

"Nothing. You can stay here with the kids and keep living your life with your sister and your late nights and whatever it was you were doing last night. I'll go to Toronto for the year. When that's done, my next posting will come, and you can come with me then. If you want to, I guess."

If I want to? This argument is getting out of control, but I'm so mad I can't even see him.

"Fine, you want to fuck off to Toronto for a year by yourself with no responsibilities or family, go ahead. We'll be here."

"No responsibilities? I must go to school, Meg! I have no choice. I have to go to Toronto so if you want to stay here, I'll just have to go alone."

"Ya, sounds rough, living in Toronto all by yourself while I keep raising your kids alone…"

"You seem to do just fine with your sister, Meg. You don't even have the kids right now!"

"It was a long night, Mark!"

"Ya, that's what you said," he responds bitterly.

I take a deep breath.

"Look, you want to drive me to Cheryl's to get the kids? Or should I call Paul?"

Grabbing his keys off the counter, he heads past me to the garage. The sweet scent of some floral perfume I've never smelled before follows him.

"Let's just go."

I wish I knew where the two of us were really headed.

28

MARK

SPRING 2007

The flight home was the worst.

After spending the week at funeral homes and planning with Dennis' mom Lori who can't seem to grasp the idea her son is gone, I'm done. The echo of the last conversation I had with my best friend, before I left for the first time with him staying home, is stuck on repeat in my head.

I should have called more. Checked in more, met him at the pub more often when he would ask. I should have made more fucking time. Instead, there's no time, and I'm here headed home after leaving him at his for good.

So much for brothers, I was barely a good enough friend.

The flight is long and with the dozen or so military on it, none of us feel like talking. We're all hung over, both from the booze after the service last night, and from the emotional drain of the entire thing. Lori can't understand, which makes sense because neither can I. How do you understand? My best friend hung himself in the closet doorway of his apartment, apparently just moments after calling the police. Best they can figure is he didn't want anyone else finding him, so he made the call and then dropped the kitchen chair. His phone was on the floor next to him, my number on the screen, but he never hit send.

My backpack feels weighted, but that's only because his medals, pins, and a beret are inside. Lori almost threw them at me. She wouldn't bury him in uniform and she didn't want any of his 'Army shit' anywhere in the house. I'll hold onto them in case she wants them back later, once she's had time.

"You think I want this shit? This is on all of you, the Army did this to him! You were there, Mark, why did you let this happen to him?"

I know she's hurting but everything she says rings true. I have no idea why he is gone and I'm still here. Why did it all break him and not me?

The girl in the seat next to me keeps leaning over, accidentally brushing up against me, trying to start a conversation. She's young, mid-twenties maybe with long red hair that keeps ending up on my shoulder and my face when she shakes her head, and far too much makeup for a six-a.m. flight. Her tits are spilling out of the little tank top she's wearing. For just a moment, the view gets to me and I let myself imagine getting lost in something soft with no consequences, just this once to ease the ache before I get home.

She keeps talking to me despite my mood. Something about going home at the end of the school year, giggling about having to get a real job now that school is done. Holy hell, I don't even want to think about how old that makes me feel. After a little while of her talking and me nodding politely, she asks the stewardess for a blanket and throws it over herself, saying something about being chilly but leaving the blanket hanging over my armrest, an invitation to share.

I stare at the blanket for a long time.

I shake my head. This has never been me. I've never even considered letting it be me. I don't want this girl next to me, I want my wife. It's a pretty stark testament to how fucked up I feel that it even crossed my mind when I've always had all I need at home.

Giving her a stunted smile, I gently brush the blanket off the armrest and put my headphones in and lean my head back, closing my eyes until I hear the flight starting its decent, my hands in my lap with my fingers twirling the thick platinum band I've worn for the last eight years.

Fuck. I need my wife.

The nap makes it worse when we arrive. I don't think I've had a decent night sleep in weeks and I barely make it to my car once the duty driver drops us off on base. I drive home in a haze but when the garage door opens, there's no car in there.

Toeing off my boots I head up the stairs, but there's no sign of her there, either. I'm taken completely off guard when I hear her voice from the living room and see her, bed hair and boots on, standing near the kitchen.

How often does she leave the kids?

Where is she going when she does?

I'm barely wrapping my head around the whole thing when our conversation takes a turn for the worse. I'm so floored by her saying she doesn't want to come with me to school in Toronto that I just answer the first way I think of. Somehow that leads to me moving alone.

In all my years in the military, I never, ever thought this would happen to us.

The words are said, though, and my pride won't take them back.

I wish I knew what I've done.

* * *

ONCE THE KIDS are in the car, I tell Megan I'll drop her off and take the kids for breakfast while she has a chance to shower and get changed. I'm trying to be helpful, but she just glares at me like I'm suggesting she walk home. I just can't win.

Instead, I spend an hour or so listening to the kids tell me about their week over the pancakes and extra bacon they order a ton of and barely touch. This time, I don't even get mad at them for it. By the time we get back, Megan is wiping down the kitchen with some yoga pants with her hair bunching wet marks on the top of a white Jack Daniels t-shirt. A few drops have fallen onto the front of the shirt, and she hasn't bothered putting on makeup or a bra.

She looks amazing.

Tori and Vince head downstairs to put on Treehouse and I sit on the stool at the island, watching her hips sway as she runs the cloth over the counter.

"I have to be at work this week," I mention. My leave has come and gone, and I have a ton of stuff to wrap up at battalion before I go.

"I know," she says without even missing a beat.

"I'll have to go fill out move paperwork. You really okay with me going alone?"

I am trying to ask nicely, trying to let her know I'll do what makes her happy. She spins around.

"I can't go…" She starts so I cut in.

"Fine. That's fine, Megan. It's just a year. I'll just go."

"Just a year…"

I don't know why she keeps staring at me like she didn't know this was how it worked, like this would happen. I don't want to move either, but it is what it is and it's not new.

"You leave, Mark, for months, training and on exercises. You come back for a bit, then it's gone half a year or more in Afghanistan. Then you come home and what? Move out for another year? So, you can be the fun dad that takes the kids out to breakfast and wrestles on the carpet and I can be the mom who makes them do homework and finish their dinner every night? Meanwhile, shit happens in my life, in our lives, and you're never there to deal with that, are you? Just with the good stuff? It's getting old, Mark!"

I open my mouth and then close it.

I don't know how to answer her. It's not that she's wrong, but she knows I'll do everything I can to be there for them if they need me, right? They've just always been good on their own. Megan's just so strong, she's never needed more. She's never needed me.

And it clicks.

She doesn't need me.

"You don't want me home?"

"That's not what I'm saying, Mark!"

"You want me to leave the Army?"

"I'm not saying that either!"

"Then what are you saying??"

"I DON'T KNOW!"

We're both breathing a little heavy, staring at each other from across the kitchen island. This time, when I open my mouth, I make one of the biggest mistakes of my life.

"Well, how about this? I turned down a job teaching a course in Gagetown before the posting because I just got back. When I get back to work, I'll accept it. I can leave next week and I'll just head to Toronto from there. Maybe we'll do better with some distance. When you know what you want, you let me know."

I regret it before I'm finished saying it, but the things about words is you can't take them back. Especially when you don't know what they really mean.

The consequences to them sometimes mean you follow through out of hurt and pride, leaving you with little wonder on how it all went wrong.

29

MEGAN

PRESENT

Mark is still sleeping on the couch.

I've been home from the hospital for days and he's barely let me out of this room, only letting the kids in to talk to me, dragging a TV up here so I can stay put.

It's driving me up the damn wall.

I must go back to work soon but he keeps putting it off, telling me I need more time. He gets the kids to school in the morning, picks them up after, and brings me dinner when he feeds them. Almost always either take-out or grilled cheese and tomato soup. I guess he learned how to parent and clean, but cooking is still a mystery. I've never minded. It's not my specialty either so I'm sure not complaining.

Not that he could hear if I did. We don't talk, not about my job other than him saying "You have time." Not about the cancer, or his deployment, or his move, or his dead best friend, or the perfume on his shirt, or the fact that he left.

We talk about the kids, permission forms and dance lessons

and lunches. We talk about laundry and the battery of the TV remote and what I want for lunch.

It was a nice break but now, I need to know where we are and where we're going. If he even still wants to go anywhere with me.

Friday night, I hear him tucking the kids in bed after they're done watching some TV up in our room. I hear the water in the kitchen and the drone of the TV from the living room. It's an hour or so later when he pokes his head in.

"I'm going to go out for a few hours with some guys from work. A couple ladies just stopped in to see how you were, you okay if they come up?"

I've had visitors, but just Cheryl and Erika. They wouldn't bother announcing their presence, either; they'd already be up here.

I take a quick glance around. I've showered today, and the sheets are pretty clean.

"Who is it?"

"It's Beth, and Cpl. Cleary's girlfriend."

I smile. I don't see them much, but they've popped by more than a few times when Mark was gone with food and wine and chats. They're always a breath of fresh air, those two.

"Sure, send them up on your way out. Let me know if you need me to pick you up," I offer.

"I can call a cab or get someone to drive me," he answers, heading down the stairs. I sigh. I'm not an invalid, and maybe I want to pick him up. He hasn't even let me go downstairs more than a handful of times, so I don't even bother arguing. I won't win.

I see Juliette's blonde hair whoosh in the room first, her tiny frame bouncing with her step, a bottle of wine in her hands. Beth is right behind her with a few glasses and a grocery bag.

"Meg! Hey! We wanted to drop these off but Maj... Mark said he was headed out and you might like some company. We don't want to intrude though so if you want us to go, just say so anytime. We aren't easily offended."

"I'd love some company."

"Yay!" Juliette sits on the corner of the bed. Looking down, she runs her hands along the quilt I have lovingly draped to the side.

"Oh! I'm so glad you like this. I know Rebecca was so happy to put a face to a recipient."

Earlier in the summer, Juliette and Beth had come to visit and Juliette had this quilt in her hands. I guess Tavish's grandmother volunteers for Victoria's Quilts, a charity full of people who lovingly make quilts for anyone undergoing chemo treatments. When Juliette had told her about me, she had been quick to send this my way and it's one of my most treasured possessions, coming with me to each treatment.

"I love it, truly. She's such an amazing lady."

"That she is." Juliette smiles, her awe of the older woman shining through. She quickly shakes her head, though, and twists off the top of the wine bottle.

"We kept it really classy, nothing but the best for you!" she jokes as she pours a few glasses. I know I can't have much at this point. I've only been back on real food for a while, but I could go for a glass and take it maybe a bit too quickly when she offers it over. She just grins.

"So, he knows now. How's that working out?" I stare at the young girl in front of me. She hasn't walked an easy road with her boyfriend, now fiancé, but they've been happily back together while he's been getting back to himself for the past six months or more. From what she's said, he's back with the company and dealing well now after giving them all quite the scare. I love her boldness. I used to think she lacked a filter but now I'm pretty sure she knows how to make small talk, she just doesn't care to.

"It's… It's good. I'm glad he knows. One day maybe we'll even talk about it!" I try to keep it light despite my frustrations.

She shakes her head.

"You are one stubborn woman."

Beth giggles while she finishes pouring for herself and sits quietly on the other corner of the bed. Her mass of black hair is up in a high ponytail, her face almost void of makeup and her skin bare to any ink, at least that I can see. With her olive skin and almond-shaped dark eyes, she looks almost the opposite to Juliette's light-hazel eyes, fair complexion, and long, poker-straight, blonde hair, but the two have been inseparable since I met them.

"You know, Megan, one of these days you're going to have to let that man take care of you."

"He can't do that and do his job, you know that."

Both ladies just look at me for a minute while Juliette picks at the label on the wine bottle. She's the first to speak up.

"When I met you, Megan, you seemed larger than life. Like this incredible example of the perfect military wife who knew all the right words and had a job and kids and a house, and managed to do it all no matter what her husband had to do. The way you came and supported Beth when Silas died? It was like you just blew in and knew exactly what to do and say. You amazed me, you know that?"

I laugh awkwardly. "I guess not anymore, hey?"

"Now, Megan? Now you're human to me. You have limits and you sometimes need a hand, and that makes you real. Even more than that, it makes you strong."

"I don't feel very strong, Juliette, and I've never been as strong as you might have thought I was."

This time Beth says something.

"Let me ask you, did you think I was weak when Juliette was there helping me when I lost Silas?"

"Of course not!"

"Me neither, I couldn't do it alone. I wasn't meant to do it alone. That's why I had friends to help me. Without Jules and eventually Jason, I don't know where I'd be. So, Megan, what the hell makes you think you're so great you don't need help sometimes, too?"

I don't have an answer for that, so I just sit and listen.

"Now I am not even married yet, so I can't be the one giving advice," Juliette starts tentatively. I wave her on.

"But I think marriage is basically the ultimate kind of friendship. And friendship doesn't work unless you lean on each other. It's not one way. Mark needs you. On top of taking care of your home and your children, you've been there for him through how much, Megan? Two, three deployments? Moves? Everything he has needed from you? Seems like he relies on you a lot, and you forgot how to rely on him. A friendship, or a marriage doesn't work like that. Something had to give."

Juliette looks at me like she's almost scared at the words she's said. Sometimes I forget she's over a decade younger than I am, especially now, when I'm worried she might be completely right.

"I don't think I know how to lean on him anymore," I whisper, staring intently at the wine in my glass like it might know the answer.

"We didn't come here to ambush you, Megan. I hope you know that. We just want to see you and Mark get through this. You're inspiring."

"I sure don't feel inspiring," I admit.

"You kidding? I've only known Tavish through one deployment, and we weren't even together for it. It was so damn hard. So hard. I can't imagine what you guys have done, all those deployments and moves and back and forth while raising kids and working and just fucking not becoming a crazy, disheveled, angry alcoholic yelling at everyone who walks by..." We all laugh, and the moment is lighter.

The girls stick around for a couple hours and we finish off the bottle of wine. Beth is still quiet, but she's comes out of her shell a little, telling stories of Silas and even a few of the new roommate they have. I'm totally blown away that these women went through what they did and on top of it all, have cared for an injured soldier who lost his leg in Afghanistan. They might think I'm inspiring, but that's beautiful. I've never met Jason, but I can only imagine he's that much better off having them on his side.

I think they can tell I'm drifting off and they say their goodbyes, promising we'll do this again soon. I'm honestly looking forward to it. These ladies may be years behind me in age, but they more than make up for it in wisdom.

As I hear the door click behind them, I start to, for probably the first time, really think through some of our marriage. From that first moment at the Greenhouse bar until now. All those sleepless nights where we'd drive around the neighbourhood to the twenty-four-hour Walmart with a screaming baby. The middle of the night phone calls from deployment where we'd have nothing to say even though it had been weeks and I'd just listen for a moment to his breathing on the other line. Driving across the country with toddlers, nights in hotel rooms with two kids on the other bed, watching TV with the sound off while they sleep and whispering to each other in the dark. The sound of his voice on the phone when he'd tell me they lost someone. The guilty relief I'd have that it wasn't him. Those homecoming kisses that took my breath away, and the incredible fact that even now, he makes my heart race and body tingle.

We've been through so much.

I guess, maybe, it's time for me to let him back in.

I wonder if that's still what he wants.

30

MARK

PRESENT

All day, I spend in that house with Megan, so close to her but not close enough. I have yet to stay with her, crashing on the couch or the floor of one of the kids' rooms. I want her more than I think I may ever have, but I don't know how to breach the space between us. So instead, I sit out like a pussy, barely talking to her, barely doing anything except the bare minimum I need to keep us both afloat.

My thoughts are a mess and every night is almost the same. I have a drink, and I think of Dennis. Then I think of how fucking mad I am at him for ending it when I had a soldier like Silas who didn't have a choice. Then I think of the day we lost Silas, and how badly I wish my best friend was here, so I could talk it over with him. Which makes me think of how mad I am at Dennis all over again. It's a vicious cycle and doesn't seem to ever stop.

I'm about to crash on the couch on Friday with beer and bad TV when I hear the quiet knock on the door. I almost don't answer, until I hear it again. It's too soft, too tentative to be a salesperson or some kind of religion peddler. I open to see a couple young ladies staring back at me.

"Hi, Mr. Lawson," the blonde, Cpl. Cleary's girl says.

"Mark," I spit out, probably not in the friendliest way.

"Hi, Mark." This time it's Elizabeth, Cpl. Jameson's widow. I'd never forget her face staring back at me.

"We came to say hi. We have a few things for Megan, but we understand if she's not up for visitors."

I just stare at them both for a while. Though they're no doubt beautiful women, my first thought is that they are *adorable,* not attractive, which makes me feel old. I decide it's time Megan and I both have a break from this non-existence with each other.

"You know what, she'd love a couple visitors for a bit. I'm heading out to the pub, but she's upstairs. I'll bring you up."

I turn around and I hear the door click behind as they walk in. I wait a moment for their shoes to come off and then start up the stairs when I feel a hand at my elbow.

"Mark, I know it's not my place, and I'm fucking terrible at this Army shit about who I can speak my mind to…"

"Juliette, I'm not your boss. You can tell me whatever you want."

She appraises me for a moment before she nods.

"Mark, I bet it's hard, to see your wife like this and take care of her. Especially since you guys have just been through a really hard time away. I know losing Silas hurt you, too. Trust me, I've been the long way around with Tav and I've seen how bad it does change you sometimes. We're here, your community, your friends are here. You might be the boss, I guess, for the guys like Tavish, but they want to help if they can. I have the night off but they're there. You should go see them."

I want to be mad at her interference but the honest care in her eyes stops me. Instead, I nod.

"I was going to head there. Thanks for visiting Meg."

I open Megan's door and let them in before letting myself out and heading to the pub.

When I arrive, Jeremy is behind the bar and it looks like Cleary and Christianson and few of the others from the company, along with one or two I don't know, are in a booth in the back.

I reconsider a moment. I was really hoping for a night of feeling sorry for myself alone with a few drinks. Something tells me that won't happen here tonight, but for whatever reason, I decide to press on.

"Hey, Jer." Jeremy gives me a chin lift as he places an already open bottle of Keith's in front of me.

"Mark. How's Megan?"

"She's doing okay, infection is gone and she's getting her strength back. She'll probably start chemo again before Christmas." The words sound more and more normal coming out of my mouth. I no longer cringe when I bite out terms like chemo and treatment. I don't know how I feel about that.

"That's great, man. Sooner she starts again, sooner you guys can put it behind ya."

I just nod, and he goes back to work behind the bar when I feel someone come up behind me and scoot into the stool next to me.

"Sir, not sure if you..."

"Matt, how about we lose the sir. We're not working."

"Sorry, Si... Mark. Shit. Okay. I'll try. Anyways, not sure if you're hoping for time alone but there's a bunch of us at the back there if you'd like to join us."

I look over at him, one of my patrol commanders. He's about the same age I was when I met Megan, though he's already got a wartime deployment behind him now. He's a good kid, looks like some hometown boy next door with his blonde hair and blue eyes and cocky grin on his face most of the time.

"Thanks, Matt," I answer sincerely, and he starts to get up as I just ask, "You must not think much of me, having to email to let me know my wife is in the hospital and I didn't even know she was sick."

Matt sits all the way back down on the stool.

"With…"

"Don't you dare even start your answer with some 'With all due respect, sir' bullshit. I'm asking a personal question, and this isn't the battalion. I just need a real answer."

There's his cocky smile back. He lets out a loud breath.

"Well, sir, I'm not married. None of the guys over there are. I mean, Tav's on his way but the rest of us, not even close. From what I hear, your wife is strong as hell. She'd have to be, knowing what the lifestyle looks like. So, I figure if she didn't want you to know, she could pull that shit off. As to why she didn't? Well, I'm not exactly in the place to give relationship advice, am I? What do I know? I don't even have a goldfish."

I chuckle and Jer leans over the bar.

"This kid is right. I mean, I've been you and what do I have to show for it? Child support payments and an ex who was shacked up with someone else before I even got home from deployment. You and Meg have been pulling this off for longer than most. I'm confident you can get through this."

I just nod. I'm glad they're confident, because I'm not.

"All right. You know what? Some company might be a good thing. Thanks."

I grab my drink and walk over to the laughing bunch in the booth. Maybe it's time I let myself be part of something again.

The night goes late. The boys tell elaborate war stories that are mostly true, and the laughter grows louder with each round of drinks. M Cpl. Sampson, who the boys have turned to calling Twiz, though they have yet to tell me why, is off by the bathrooms with a leggy redhead about five minutes from an indecent exposure charge. I've noticed Cleary is still nursing the same beer he was when I sat down. His eyes are clearer and he's smiling again. He and the giant-sized tanker argue over fitness tests.

"Fine, you and your giant tree trunk arms might beat me in an arm wrestle, but I could beat you in a foot race any day!"

"I'd like to see that!" Twiz calls from the hall over his redhead's shoulder.

"It's easy. First step, hide his damn bionic foot. Let's see him catch up to me then!"

Everyone laughs; soldiers have the kind of dark humour that can laugh about an amputation, and I glance around wondering what it all might sound like to an outsider. I guess it doesn't much matter, though. This family right here is what's keeping these guys together. Who cares what anyone else thinks. The way they include me in the conversation while they talk with honest happiness about Cpl. Jameson, it starts to heal that part of me that will always hold onto my responsibility for his death. It's clear, just by their willingness to let me sit here while they reminisce, they don't see it that way. It's a lot for me to take in.

It's getting late in the evening when Matt looks over at me. They had just been telling the story of Silas and Tavish using gun tape to attach some poor private to his bunk right before the usual rocket attack time, and I had just been jokingly telling them how they need to not tell me this shit, when he asks me exactly the question I was avoiding.

"You were close with Captain Staley, weren't you?"

The table quiets and they all look over. It was no secret at battalion what happened to Dennis. A dead serving member, that's big news. For many of the new guys, there were I'm sure a lot of whispers and questions.

"I was." I can't think of anything else to say.

"That's a pretty fucked-up situation, that is," Matt adds.

"No, what happened to Cpl, Jameson was fucked up. What

Dennis did was fucking bullshit." I put my beer down more forcefully than I intended and all eyes end up on me.

"I'm a, I'm gonna grab some air."

I beeline for the exit like my life depends on it. Out the door, I lean back against the building and let out a long, slow breath and close my eyes. It feels wrong, equating what Dennis did to what happened to one of my soldiers at war. Cpl. Jameson fought for his life and Dennis, he just gave his up. I'm sure to the guys inside, the ones who have only seen him these last few years, he was a broody, pissy, powder-keg and a poor example of a leader at best. They'll never meet the Dennis who had my back in Kosovo, the one who caused shit with me in Guam. They won't have the chance to ever meet the roommate that would bang on my door in the morning with coffee already made, or who single-handedly got me through half of my military college courses with countless late nights of coffee and patience.

Dennis hadn't been that guy in more than a few years, if I let myself admit it, and that makes me feel even worse.

I open my eyes when I hear the door to the pub open. Cleary glances my way and walks over, leaning his back next to me on the wall.

"Did M... Lt. Christianson ever tell you anything about me when I first got back, sir?"

"Let's not start with the formalities now, Tavish. I've had too much to drink to listen to all the rank and sir bullshit."

Tavish chuckles. "Fair enough. Did Matt ever tell you what a head case I was?"

I glance over at him. He looks so much better than that one afternoon coming off the bus. He's gained back some weight and his eyes don't look like they're being held down by weights. He holds his shoulders up again.

"I followed that he was keeping track of you, but he kept the details in confidence," I admit.

"Huh." Another deep breath. "He did his best, you know, just trying to gently get me out there, see other guys, not wallow in my room. I was too far gone, though. So, the time he really had it out with me? He found a gun along with a few notes I'd written on a particularly bad night in my drawer."

I straighten up and raise my eyebrows at him.

"I never had a real plan, or even a real desire to off myself. At least not at that point. What I'm trying to say, though, is I guess I know how you get there."

He lets that sink in for a moment in comfortable silence.

"You're standing here, though."

"I am. I'm good. I don't have as many nightmares now, and the guilt doesn't paralyse me anymore. It took work, though. And support, therapy, my friends, and my girl…"

"I should have done something for Dennis."

"Let me ask you something. Did you tie the rope around his neck?"

I just stare at him, stunned. What the hell kind of question is that?

"Because if you didn't, you aren't responsible for his death. Could there have been one thing you might have done to have helped him before that? One more phone call, one more message, one more night out? Who knows. Would he have gotten help that forty-seventh time you asked if you would have done it? There's no way to know if he ever would have chosen to get better. And that's the key, you couldn't have made him no matter how many times you tried.

"I know what it's like to lose your best friend. And to think, maybe there was something I could have done. That's all I thought about after the IED killed Silas. I could have switched and driven that day. Or maybe I could have gotten to him in the vehicle sooner to get him out, or maybe if I would have watched the bank closer, I would have seen something and warned them… so many maybes.

"They mean nothing. Because I can't go back to change a thing and reality is in the end, I didn't set the IED and I didn't plan the ambush. So, I am not responsible for his death. And neither are you. For either of them."

In that moment, it's like even the cars on the street and the buzz of the sign know to be silent and all I hear is my heart in my chest.

"I guess what I wanted to say was that I hope you can forgive your friend. What he did was fucked up, but I think I can see it from his side enough to know he didn't want to hurt anyone. He just wanted to stop his own pain."

"You know, Cleary, I'm supposed to be the one who gives you all the advice," I say as I let out the breath I didn't know I was holding.

"Tell you what. Monday, if I see you at work, I'll salute with one hand in my pocket and you can make yourself feel better by advising me all the ways you'll kick my ass."

I lean my hands on my knees, laughing while I hear the rest of the group pile out to head home.

"Can I give you a ride? I have a feeling Jules and Beth are probably just on their way back anyways."

"Just because we had a moment here doesn't mean I'm ready to ride bitch on the back of your bike, Cleary."

He shakes his head smiling and then nods towards a truck.

"It's fucking cold out, sir. My ride is put away for the winter. Anyways, I think you're right close to my condo."

I say goodbye to all the guys and climb into his truck.

Looks like I've just been schooled by a kid a good decade younger than me.

Now, to see if I can win over my own wife.

"I just need to make one stop on the way home. Where's the closest Mac's?"

31

MEGAN

PRESENT

When I wake up, I can tell almost immediately I'm not alone before I even open my eyes. I keep them closed for a moment. I can feel his gaze on me, his hand on my hip. He used to do this all the time when we started dating, watch me while I slept. Most of the time I was awake, but I loved it so much, I would just keep still.

"I always knew when you were awake; your breathing changes," he whispers. I smile and open my eyes.

"Why didn't you say anything?"

"Because I liked looking at you."

"And now?"

"I haven't done it enough. I haven't done anything enough."

I sit up, propping myself with an elbow to look at him lying next to me. "You do plenty."

He just smiles sadly. Then he reaches to the bedside table and grabs a slushie and a bag of penny candies, passing them over. My laugh comes out more as a snort as I take a sip of the sickly sweet drink.

"Why didn't you tell me, Megan?"

I sit up a little farther. I guess I knew we had to talk about this sooner or later. I pull myself to sitting, but he grabs my hips and brings me back so I lie looking at him.

"No hiding. Why didn't you tell me?"

I take my time to grab a green frog from the candy bag and shove it in my mouth, chewing slowly before I answer.

"It's not that I tried to keep it from you! It's just that when I first found the lump, you were in Afghanistan and before I could tell you about the biopsy, Dennis died, and you were gone. Then you came home smelling like perfume and I didn't know what to say. Suddenly, you were moving, and it was all too late!"

I blurt it out in one big run on words and Mark is left looking at me more than a little confused.

"Wait... perfume?"

"When you came home from the funeral, you said how you could move all alone and then I could smell perfume on you, and I didn't know what I should think."

Mark blinks, his face scrunched up for a moment in thought.

"You mean the morning I came home before eight a.m. and you looked like you just got back in the clothes you slept in? I didn't know why you didn't have the kids, or where you'd been..."

"Well, if you would have asked, you would have known I had just found out for sure I had cancer and after we went over my treatment plan with the doctor, I drank wine with Erika at Cheryl's place. When I came home, the kids were already in bed there, so they stayed. I was so terrified I cried myself to sleep alone on the couch without even taking my boots off. It was one of the worst nights of my life."

His face drops.

"Well, if you would have asked me, I would have said there was a lady next to me on the plane who got a little too friendly, so I had to put in my headphones and ignore her while trying my best to flaunt my ring in front of her face like a crazy man."

That makes me smile just a little, and I shake my head.

"We've been married too long and been through too much that we would end up living apart because we're both too stupid to have a single conversation."

"I didn't want to go without you. I just didn't want to push when you said you didn't want to go."

"I didn't want to go because I knew I was starting treatment here... I thought you'd ask me why."

"I didn't ask why because I was scared the answer was just that you didn't need me anymore."

"I didn't fight it because I was scared you'd say you were leaving for good. Mostly, I was just scared, Mark. I have cancer and I'm scared."

Mark scoops me up into him where I just relax against his chest for the longest time.

"After I lost Silas, and then came home and Dennis was gone... I didn't feel like I had the right to lead this family, Megan. I failed over and over. You don't need me anymore." His voice is quiet as he speaks into my hair.

"Mark, you haven't failed anyone. Not your soldiers and not your family. I'm sorry I got so wrapped up in taking care of myself I let you think that it's because you aren't good enough. It was always because I learned to handle it all when you were gone and I forgot how to let it go when you weren't. I don't just need you, Mark, I want you. Always."

We sit a little while longer before I admit it all. "I lost myself somewhere. When I was diagnosed... I was worried that meant I would never have the chance to find me again."

Mark holds me tighter.

"I'm here and we'll do this together. WE are going to get through this together. I know you're scared, but I've got you. When we see the other side, and we will, the next step is making sure you get to be you again. Whatever that takes."

The tears come for a while before I relax, and he continues to run his hand up and down from mid-thigh to my ribcage, over and over.

"We're fucking idiots, the two of us, aren't we?"

Right now, it's been so long and all I can concentrate on is his fingers lightly touching the underside of my breasts each time they venture under my sleep shirt.

"Mhmm." Cocking his head at my answer, Mark takes a good look at me in the light that's just coming in from under the curtains. It must be early.

"I haven't had you in so long, Meg..."

"I'm here now..." My breath is now coming in embarrassingly quick gasps and his fingers continue to explore from the outside of my thighs to under my breasts and down my soft stomach to the apex of my thighs. Just teasing until my hips rock towards him with the touch. I can see by the substantial bulge in his boxer shorts in front of me that I'm not the only one feeling it. I reach with one hand, freeing him from the shorts before swinging one leg over his hips until his back is on the bed and my naked center rubs over him.

In one move, his hand is on the small of my back and his knees trap mine. He has me on my back and my legs wrapped around his hips. Leaning forward so one hand meets the mattress next to my head, he uses his other to guide himself inside me. The slow burn after this long quickly turns to pleasure until he has my hands and his above my head while he rocks into me.

"Mine. Mine. Mine," he whispers in my ear like a mantra as

his pace quickens. Taking one of my hands in his, he pushes it between us and the added friction has me pushing hard to my own release, only moments before I hear him finally let himself go, calling my name when he does.

Collapsing on top of me, panting heavily in my ear, I hear him whisper one more time.

"Mine."

We both manage to drift back to sleep, still connected but completely content.

* * *

"C'mon, Meg, let's go."

It's been almost a month since I got home from the hospital and I am set to restart chemo tomorrow. I told Mark I would go ahead and shave my head this time. I had been putting it off, mostly because it would have made everything that much more real. This time, I don't want to watch it fall out so I asked him to shave it for me tonight. He agreed, even though I know it's going to be so hard for him. He decided we would head out on the town one more time before I did it. Hiring the thirteen-year-old girl next door so she can watch our TV while the kids are already in bed, we opted to grab a late dinner and drinks at the pub instead of anything fancy. I'm more of a jeans girl and I'll take comfortable over most else these days.

"I don't know what your rush is, the pub will still be there in five minutes."

We may have talked through a lot this past while, but I will never conform to his crazy need to be everywhere early. I have lots of time.

Mark gives me a swat on the butt when I finally get down the stairs and step through the door he holds open. "You're killing me, woman!"

"Mark, it's the Crown. It's not like we had to reserve a table on a Sunday night. Relax!"

He smiles as he starts the car. "I just want you to have a good night, doll."

I put my hand over his on the shifter.

"Thank you."

When we pull up to the parking lot, there are more cars there than I'd expect, but it's the sign on the door that throws me.

"We might need to make new plans, Mark. Looks like there's a private party here tonight."

"Oh ya?" Mark opens the door undeterred and I reach out and grab his arm when I step through.

Cheryl and Erika sit among a pile of pink balloons up at the front by the bar. Juliette and Beth too. I see more than a few of Mark's friends from work, along with Jeremy, lining the walls and chairs to the side.

In the middle of the room is one of the big chairs from a table that's usually in the back. It's sitting on top of what looks like a plastic tablecloth.

Cheryl is the first to speak up, while I just stare, eyes wide.

"This time, we're all in this together, sis. All of us. So, we take this one step at a time together, too. Starting with this one."

Cheryl sits in the chair and I haven't even registered what's happening or why everyone is here before I hear the buzzing of a razor.

"Cheryl!' A half laugh, half sob comes out of my mouth and Mark squeezes me from behind.

"It's just hair, Megs." She winks at me as the first chunk of her blonde mane hits the ground. Paul, holding the razor behind her, winces.

"Yup, it's just hair…" His voice is much less reassured, and everyone laughs.

I loosen Mark's grip on me and walk up to Cheryl,

crouching down to look her in the eye. I can't even begin to stop the tears from falling.

"Stop that! You know I'd do anything for you!" Cheryl spits out in a half sob and soon, we're both crying while Paul attempts to get the clippers across her scalp.

She leans in and whispers in my ear, "I'm not the only one."

I look over and see Erika approaching one of the soldiers I recognize from Mark's work. He has black hair that seems a little too long, and hard blue eyes.

"Hey, she's gonna take forever. Care to help me get started?" He grins.

"Seems like a shame to cut off this gorgeous hair, but you've got an awfully pretty… face… so it's a deal."

Erika grins and winks, and the two of them pull a chair onto the plastic cloth. As I look around, I see they aren't the only ones. Suddenly, I'm standing in the middle watching while Cheryl, Erika, Juliette, and Beth sit down, and their hair falls to the floor.

It's all I can do to just stand there, crying, with no chance of any coherent thought coming out. Soon, everyone laughs and talks while the hair piles up. Jeremy comes around with beer and shots.

"Figured I'd make myself useful since I didn't have any hair to offer." He winks at me, the sweat on his head making it shine in the light from the bar and I laugh.

"Thank you so much," is all I can squeak out and he just squeezes my shoulder.

"You have a much bigger family than you think."

Soon, all but Beth are done, a mass of hair tangled on the plastic covering the floor. "This is taking *forever*!" the huge, dark-skinned man with the razor says while buzzing another section. He's not wrong, even after they cut it shorter to make it easier, Beth has a lot of hair and it's not going quietly.

"Oh shush, you big baby. Now you don't have to complain about my hair getting everywhere in the house!"

"One time! One time I pointed out maybe I'd like a meal without one of your hairs in it…"

I laugh, and Juliette comes up from behind me.

"You know, this is going to make my mornings so much easier!" she says with a grin, rubbing her hand on her buzzed head.

"It's a good thing I love you, baldy. This is going to take some getting used to!" Her fiancé buries his face into her neck from behind and she melts into him.

"All right, which one of you has the guts?" A booming voice calls out from one of the chairs and I turn to see Bill, Mark's old sergeant major, sitting down holding a smaller pair of clippers. He doesn't really have any hair on his head so I'm not sure what he means for a moment and by the time I do, there's already a scramble. Tavish makes it to the razor first.

"Well, sir, if you insist…"

"Get it done, Cleary," he growls, jokingly I hope. Tavish doesn't seem deterred, anyways, and it takes only moments for the long, waxed mustache to vanish.

"Oh my, Bill! You look like a teenager!" I giggle despite my best efforts not to. His face without the iconic moustache looks decades younger.

"I think it will take more than a clipping to take that many decades off, ma'am, but I'll still take it as a compliment."

He stands and pulls the clippers from Tavish's hands.

"I'll take these back, Cleary. Who knows what you'd do with them…"

Tavish just laughs and I see Erika and Cheryl sweeping the big piles of hair. Then Mark pulls two chairs up to the middle of the sheet.

"All right, doll. It's just me and you."

I just stare a moment at this man. My partner. My best friend. I can't believe I thought, even for a moment, I could do any of this without him. Even if he hasn't been beside me the whole way physically, he's always had my back. Always.

I plop down into the chair facing his, Cheryl behind me and Paul behind Mark. He reaches out to hold my hands in his between us as I hear the clippers buzz.

"Together, babe. We've got this together."

EPILOGUE

MARK

SPRING 2009

*J*umping out of a plane sounded like a good idea at the time.

Up here at twelve thousand feet, however, I am forced to remember why I stuck with being a light infantry soldier and not an airborne one.

Because planes were meant to fly in, not jump out of.

I needed to do something. Put these last months and months of hurt behind us and let it all go. Accept the things that cannot be changed and move forward. That's what the experts would say, right? That I need to let go?

The look on Megan's face sitting in front of me in the back of this tiny plane assures me this was the right call.

With the kids at Cheryl's for the week, I decide to take Megan to Vegas to celebrate finishing her final chemo treatment. Somehow, on the way to planning this all while sitting at her bedside during her treatments, we planned this part, too.

Skydiving over the Grand Canyon. A true testament to all I would do for her, because right now? I want to shake the guy who straps me to his chest and make him fly me back to solid ground.

Except I'm supposed to be the tough one here. Instead, I give her the best 'let's do this' grin I can muster before I watch her and her partner disappear out the side of the plane, her excited screams following her.

"We're up next," the way-too-happy asshole who I've watched jump with like five other people this morning says as he scoots us to the edge. I can't decide if I'm happy to know he's jumped that many times safely, or if I'm starting to worry about statistics and percentages.

I don't have time, though; he doesn't even give me a countdown before he pushes us off the edge of the plane and into the waiting sky.

As much as I'm sure this will end me, that my obituary will read three deployments and then death by vacation skydiving accident, we don't plummet to our death. We fall only moments before we're jerked back and begin to float.

"It always amazes me how some of you military guys would jump into incoming fire but not jump out of a plane," he jokes behind me.

"I'm better at shooting than flying," I mutter, and he just laughs.

"We're flying just fine right now."

I glance around and see what I think is Megan off a little below us.

"You and your wife celebrating an anniversary here?" he asks, probably to distract me from the still significant distance between me and the ground.

"No anniversary. We're celebrating her finishing cancer treatments."

"No shit? That's a tough woman you got there. Good to hear."

He has no idea.

We float the rest of the way quietly and eventually, I can enjoy the view as long as I don't think about the fall. Still, when we land on solid ground, I'm damn happy. Megan rushes up to me almost the moment I'm out of my gear.

"Mark! That was amazing!"

I just grin. I'd give this woman anything, apparently.

THAT NIGHT, I drag her down the strip and into a tiny chapel. We're laughing, probably half due to the hilarious street preacher yelling on the sidewalk and half due to the number of margaritas we've drank on our way down. When we duck inside, though, we do our best to be quiet as I pull her with me against the wall in the back to watch a classic Vegas ceremony already in progress. A little thing with short, cropped, blonde hair and a white sundress holds hands with a tall, dark-haired soldier in jeans as they stand in front of a badly dressed officiant speaking in a terrible, fake Southern accent.

The bride's attendant has the same short haircut, her dark strands a mass of short, unruly waves on her head. There's three more men rounding off the little audience of four. They're all stage whispering and giggling loudly, but no one minds. It's the happiest wedding I think I've ever seen.

Their laughter as they slide on the rings and he kisses her for far longer than appropriate is heartwarming. Megan's tears fall quick down her face as she slides off the funky red wig she'd put on earlier. Her fine blonde hair is barely at her ears and sticks out everywhere, sweaty from under the wig in the Nevada heat. When the bride and groom turn around, they catch our eye and grin. Megan gives a little wave, the smile on her face brighter than I've seen in… longer than I care to think about. I lean into her ear.

"What do you say, Mrs. Lawson? This time, next year, our tenth anniversary we make this re-official? Just like this?"

She squeezes my hand.

"I wouldn't want to be anywhere else."

SNEAK PEEK

RUN FROM HOME

It's far hotter in this bed than it should be.

That's my first thought when I come to consciousness. My room in the condo is always cool, and I sleep with the window open even in the winter. Right now, though, I'm burning up. The blanket covering me is heavy and way too hot. My head feels like there's a ping pong game being played behind my eyelids. I try to scramble together memories about the night before, but nothing seems to stick.

I will myself to peel open my sandpaper eyelids and realize it's not a blanket covering me at all. It's a woman and judging by the soft comforter and purple wall colour, I'm at her place.

She's still asleep, I can feel her rhythmic breathing against my chest. One of her slender arms is thrown across my waist. My naked waist.

I quick glance down and I can see neither of us have anything on. Not that I'd complain about that, she has a slim, athletic build with pale, white skin that's dotted with freckles. A redhead. I smile.

I love redheads.

I shift just slightly so I can see her head and confirm my suspicion.

Except I can't. She must be a redhead, but she has nothing but soft stubble on her head. It's shaved completely bald.

That's when the previous night rushes back to me. At the pub, we were meeting in support of Major Lawson's wife who was re-starting her chemo treatments. The women all shaved their heads, Tav's girl Jules, Silas' widow Beth, and two others. Megan's sister, and her best friend. What was her name?

Erika. She was a gorgeous redhead until she sauntered up and asked me to help her shave her head. Then she was just plain gorgeous, even without the hair. The party continued after that. Shots, tequila... I think. Erika went drink for drink with me, not an easy feat since I must outweigh her by almost a hundred pounds and have hard drinking down to an art. She didn't seem any worse for wear than I was, though.

We shared a cab. I remember her pressed up against me in it when we decided to only make one stop. After that, I'm surprised we even made it into her bed. I'm pretty sure we made more than a few pit stops. The hall. The kitchen.

The kitchen table. Even hungover, my body immediately reacts to the memory of spreading her out on that kitchen table. She was exactly what I love in a woman; definitely no passive participant, she more than gave as good as she got.

More than once.

I squeeze my eyes shut a moment and will it all down. It doesn't matter how hot she is, I don't do mornings. Ever. I need to get out of here

It takes me a good five minutes to slowly extract myself from underneath Erika's sleeping form without waking her. It's an art I've mostly perfected, getting out from underneath a woman and on my way before she can wake and ask me for more.

One night, a few laughs, hot sex, and a quick getaway. That's all I ever do. I never promise more, I'm not a monster, I'm always honest that it's just because I don't have more in me to give. This is who I am and what I do. Even sitting as close to thirty as I am, it's never changed. If anything, it's become even more ingrained in me.

I can't give them more when I don't have it in me to give.

This works in my life. And with pre-deployment training coming up and another trip to Afghanistan on the horizon, more than ever a quick exit is the best option. No matter the laughs, or how good the sex.

And holy shit, it was... amazing.

Once I'm off the bed, I take another long moment to enjoy Erika's sleeping figure. She's on her stomach, the blanket sitting just below where her back slopes to her ass. The freckles on her shoulders trail down the slight indent of her spine. I can't see her face since she's got it buried into a pillow, but I find myself smiling at the slightly uneven buzz cut, a few errant strands still hang in a few places.

I won't be giving up my day job to take up as a barber, apparently.

Grabbing my jeans and t-shirt from the night before, I can smell booze and a woman's scent lingering on them as I slip into them as quietly as I can and attempt to soften the click when I open the door.

"Ah... Twiz was it?" I hear muffled behind me.

Shit.

I turn, bracing myself for the inevitable 'you asshole sneaking out without saying goodbye' lecture. Instead, Erika rolls onto her back, not bothering to pull up the blanket, and I'm the one almost convinced to stay at the sight in front of me.

"Ya?"

"Hit the button on the coffee maker on the way out, would ya?" She waves one hand in the direction of the door before rolling again to the side and closing her eyes.

It's sheer mechanics that gets me down the hall and into the kitchen where I find a pre-set coffee maker. I press the button and head out, taking only a final glance at that kitchen table before I close the door behind me.

Huh.

The one woman who doesn't seem to care to see me walk out the door in the morning and for the first time in as long as I can remember, I almost want to stay.

MORE BY KIM MILLS

THE WAY HOME SERIES

>All The Way Home *(Tavish and Juliette)*
>Run From Home *(Twiz and Erika)*
>Broken Home *(Jeremy and Jordyn)*
>
>COMING SOON
>
>The Long Way Home *(Bill and Patricia)*
>Carry Me Home *(Matt and Sarah)*

THE WHAT I NEED SERIES

>Harder Than It Should Be *(Lincoln and Abby)*

DEAR READER

Mark, Megan and Dennis are fictional characters, but the realities of deployment, reintegration and mental health issues among military members and their families is definitely not. Suicide has cost more military lives than the War in Afghanistan did, and it's an enemy that can be much harder to fight.

If you feel like you're drowning I encourage you, most of all, to reach out to the support network in front of you. Whether it's family, friends or your military community, let someone in. Finding solid ground again is just that much easier when you're not out their flailing on your own.

If you are a military member, veteran, or the family of one and you don't know where to turn, there are resources out there for you.

(Canada) The Family Info Line (24/7)
1-800-866-4546
(Canada) The Member Assistance Program (24/7)
1-800-567-5803

(USA) Military OneSource (24/7)

DEAR READER

1-800-273-8255 and Press 1

(England) Combat Stress (24/7)
0800-138-1619

(Australia) National Welfare Coordination Center (24/7)
1800-801-026

Remember, seeking help is not a sign of weakness. It is the strongest thing you can do for yourself and those who love you.

ACKNOWLEDGMENTS

I am still here but by the grace of my God, and forever grateful that His mercies are new each morning because I never fail to need them.

To Dh. You've put up with a level of crazy this year that surpasses any reasonable person's patience. You've never wavered. I will never not be grateful for the way you love me.

For all my *She is Fierce* readers, you guys are the real heroes. You made this happen and I couldn't have done it without you all. A special thank you goes to those who have answered specific questions for me, especially Kevin Martin, whose descriptions of his experiences in Kosovo helped me shape that part of this story.

For my Beta Reader group, you rock. You rock at eleven at night when I need readers, you rock at six a.m. when I'm harassing you for your thoughts, and your feedback and encouragement is what made any of this worth reading.

I'm still an armoured soldier's spouse who writes a series about infantry soldiers. Dh continues to answer my infantry questions with "I don't know, *Kim*, why don't you ask a *Patricia*," and so far, none of our Dirty Patricia friends have blocked my number.

To all our military family who continues, year after year, to answer my questions and put up with my writing over the years, I am showing my appreciation the way I know you'd want it: By keeping your damn name out of it.

ABOUT THE AUTHOR

The Fight for Home is the second novel for writer Kim Mills, the author of the Canadian military family blog *She is Fierce*. Kim has been married to her high school sweetheart for over 16 years and together they have 3 children. You can find the five of them, along with their dog Trooper, at home wherever the army sends them.

You can find Kim on social media:

Made in the USA
Middletown, DE
29 August 2022